I0634206

SHORT STORIES

SYDNEY SCHOOL OF ARTS

First print edition: Sydney 2019
First ebook edition: Sydney 2019
Publisher: Sydney School of Arts & Humanities
15-17 Argyle Place Millers Point NSW 2000
www.ssoa.com.au

Short Stories Sydney School of Arts
ISBN 9978-0-6487505-0-5 (print book)
ISBN 9978-0-6487505-1-2 (ebook)

Copyright ©Editors: Christine Williams & Sharon Dean©Contributors: David Benn / Gabriela Dimitrova / Kay Dunne / Lawrence Goodstone / Richard Hambleton / Jody Harper / Sam Herzog / Carole Ingram / Matt Jackson / Jennifer Neil / Theo Perry / Jim Piotrowski / Michelle Porter / Wil Roach / Patricia Ruell / Faisal Sayani / Graham Wilson, 2019.

The moral rights of the above authors being identified as authors of single stories included in this work have been asserted in accordance with the Copyright, Designs and Patents Act, 1988. All rights reserved. Without limiting the rights under copyright reserved above, no part of this publication may be reproduced, stored in or introduced into a retrieval system, or transmitted, in any form or by any means (electronic, mechanical, photocopying, recording or otherwise), without the prior written permission of both the particular copyright owner above and the publisher, Sydney School of Arts & Humanities. Nor may it be otherwise circulated in any form of binding or with any cover other than that in which it is published by this publisher as an ebook or a print book, without a similar condition being imposed on the subsequent purchaser.

This is a work of fiction. Names, characters, businesses, organisations, places and incidents are either the product of the authors' imaginations or are used fictitiously. Any resemblance to actual persons, living or dead, events, or locales is entirely coincidental.

Cover design and formatting Ferdinando Manzo.
Typeset Times New Roman

Printed and bound by Lightning Source, 2019.
National Library of Australia Cataloguing-in-Publication data:
Short Stories Sydney School of Arts / Editors: Williams, Christine &
Dean, Sharon. Contributors: David Benn / Gabriela Dimitrova / Kay
Dunne / Lawrence Goodstone / Richard Hambleton / Jody Harper /
Sam Herzog / Carole Ingram / Matt Jackson / Jennifer Neil / Theo
Perry / Jim Piotrowski / Michelle Porter / Wil Roach / Patricia Ruell
/ Faisal Sayani / Graham Wilson, 2019.
ISBN 9978-0-6487505-0-5 (print book)
ISBN 9978-0-6487505-1-2 (ebook)

Contents

FOREWORD

When the time arrives to begin to collate the stories which will comprise the body of text for Sydney School of Arts & Humanities' annual anthology, a feeling of excitement coupled with a sense of composure can almost overwhelm me. It's a combination of these sensations that I identify with the necessity to carry out a balancing act unlike any other. Sure, it's not as difficult as walking a high wire at the circus, I imagine, but nevertheless there's plenty at stake.

First, the feelings of writers who have submitted offerings and may be refused. As editors, we must not be too dismissive if the introduction to a story doesn't immediately appeal. Second, recognition of the just reward of publication is paramount for those writers who have succeeded as storytellers, at least initially, by charming the editors. We test taste, then go on to consume for flavour, texture, freshness and overall produce quality. We take our responsibilities as siphons to the general public seriously, politely discarding, behind closed doors, the unsavoury or even rank.

The measure of a story must take into account basic skills such as punctuation and grammar, as well as other vital elements: purpose set and fulfilled, general appeal of the subject, plot development, character exposition, appropriate and consistent narrative style, cultural accord, non-discriminative practice relating to gender, race or disability recognition, other legal considerations, iconoclastic or satiric issues, contemporaneity, diaphaneity, spontaneity, omneity (or close to it, considering the restrictions of a single call for submissions) ... Phew! There's a lot to it. Blood pressure, sweaty brows and tearful recriminations may follow.

So, here we are at the end of the culling and editing road, with a collection of stories we – glorious authors and humble editors all – are proud to have produced for presentation to the mainstream reading public.

Read on to experience all of the following anecdotal views: Faisal Sayani's appraisal of possible consequences from couchsurfing; Jennifer Neil's warning of repercussions from rollerskating; Jim Piotrowski's experience of the highlights of a nun's jubilee celebration.

Other stories have a sexy bent: Michelle Porter ponders 'Will I or won't I?'; Ric Hambleton features a slimming style of underwear; Kay Dunne describes an unexpected encounter; Lawrence Goodstone sets up a dilemma resulting from a decades-long marriage.

That's not to say that serious subjects or travel to distant cultures aren't also covered in this collection. Gabriela Dimitrova takes us to Napoleonic France, Patricia Ruell describes a family's privations in wartime Poland, David Benn looks at the significance of building sandcastles on the Gold Coast, and Wil Roach considers the symbolism of a hessian dress in Trinidad. Matt Jackson offers us insight into a male relationship; Theo Perry looks at why some people agonise over religion; Jody Harper explores the sobering effects of drought in far western New South Wales; Carole Ingram shows us second sight can be the sweetest; and Graham Wilson leads us into the mysterious history of a sandstone house in Sydney.

Perhaps the 'pièce de résistance' of the anthology, however, is Sam Herzog's tale set mainly in a bar where, just as in any bar in the world, you're likely to meet an eccentric character or two.

All products of expansive imaginative scope, these stories are at once thought-provoking and viscerally charged. We hope you can set aside some 'me time' to fully enjoy these short fiction escapades and even pass on our authors' tidbits of delight for others to savour.

Dr Christine Williams with Dr Sharon Dean – Editors
Ferdinando Manzo – Text Formatting and Cover Design

COUCHSURFING

Faisal Sayani

Amy walked into the newsroom with a tiny bawling infant in her arms. The child's voice was quickly drowned out by the sound of the screaming television sets spewing out live news from competitors' networks. It was around 8 pm, the crunch time for a television news business in Karachi.

Najam, an executive producer, was on the phone with one of his producers in the control room of a studio where a live talk show was hitting the airwaves. 'I'll talk to you later,' he said to the producer in a muffled voice before hanging up.

He strode towards Amy as she took tentative steps in his direction. His questioning eyes met her evasive eyes and she looked away. Just then, Alia, a show host, emerged from nowhere and found a spot between Amy and Najam.

'Boss, she is hungry. You need to get her baby formula and a bottle … and ... and some clothes. She doesn't have any.'

Alia was just being her usual overdramatic self. He hated her excessive use of 'boss'. The producer, Ahmed, was standing furthest away from Najam in this small and loud congregation, which had started to look like a queue, of sorts.

'I tried telling you ... over the phone,' Ahmed stammered.

Najam glared at him. 'But how can they just hand over a baby to you? Isn't there a strict and lengthy procedure in place? I was told that people wait for years before they get a go-ahead for adoption.'

'Yes, it's not easy, boss. But we convinced her.' Alia was full of enthusiasm, like a child expecting a reward for having achieved an impossible task.

'You convinced the director of The Foundation?' Najam exclaimed in disbelief. 'Isn't she a bit of a hard nut?'

'But she loves our show and is a friend of mine too. I told her Amy is like your family. She trusts us, boss.'

Najam chewed over each word. 'She is not my family! She's a single woman who doesn't even live in this country.'

'That's why. The director thought the child would have a better future in America.' Alia's zeal began to fade and she looked into Amy's eyes, confused. 'She interviewed Amy thoroughly, boss.'

Annoyed and exhausted, Najam looked at the newborn, which hadn't stopped screaming all the while. He was aware of the magnitude of the prying eyes around him. Reporters, editors, cameramen, technicians – there must have been at least fifty people in the newsroom. Being the executive producer, he had to act responsibly, he thought. So, controlling his rage, he picked up the car keys from his desk and signalled Amy with his eyes to follow him.

Not a word was uttered by either of them to each other for over an hour. Not until they were returning to his apartment from the supermarket. Both were shocked. Each had his and her reasons. *What the fuck was she thinking?*

Najam considered the several incidents associated with the new form of casual accommodation called couchsurfing, an online social networking service for free home-stays. A Pakistani friend of his who'd migrated to Germany had shared with him a couple of interesting experiences that she'd had with couchsurfers she'd hosted in her tiny apartment in Leipzig. She liked meeting people from different backgrounds and it all went well for her except for one instance when one dude insisted on roaming around naked in the flat, which she wasn't very comfortable about.

I can handle naked bodies, he'd reasoned, and signed himself up. It was quite surprising for him to see a significant number of members in Pakistan. There was even a WhatsApp group out there and they were meeting quite regularly at these fancy roadside tea places that had just mushroomed in every other corner of the upscale estate of Karachi. Being a private person, he was reluctant to put the pictures of his abode on the website, but with some encouragement offered from the Leipziger, he went ahead with the process of welcoming absolute strangers to his cherished apartment. It had only been six months since his divorce. At first, it had been hard to live alone but very recently he'd begun to enjoy his own company. *The late thirties is not so late, is it?* Only now he noticed the magnificence of the vast Arabian Sea from his cosy lounge after several years of having lived there. *Perhaps it's time to share this view*, he thought.

A complete stranger, Amy had a simple but interesting profile on *Couchsurfing* – as a thirty-three-year-old freelance photographer born and raised in the USA. Although half of her face on her display photo was hidden behind a giant camera lens, it wasn't hard to tell that she had South-Asian roots. It was during her nineteen days stay at his place he learned that her grandparents still lived in Karachi. She came across as a kind of activist. For instance, she had a photo of a pile of books which included *My Feudal Lord.* Najam thought: *So we have at least one book in common.* He was scanning her profile because she'd sent him a request for a homestay. For nineteen nights. He hesitated briefly and clicked the green bar that read: 'Accept'.

They quickly moved to the intimate WhatsApp and Facebook messaging from the formal Couchsurfing communication. Years later, when Najam was going through the texts they wrote to each other before she arrived in Karachi, he found them to be rather cheesy.

Najam: So, are you coming?

Amy: I am. Just sorting tickets. Looking at the second week of next month. Is that a good time for u?

Najam: Yeah sure. I'm here only.

Amy: Need anything from Africa?

Najam: Africa? I thought you lived in Milwaukee.

Amy: I do. I am working on a project in Zanzibar at the moment.

Najam: How is it like there?

Amy: Pretty amazing. Blue waters. White sands. Perfect weather. Yummy food. Highly recommend this place for a honeymoon ;)

Najam: Will keep that in mind :)

***

Amy: Got the ticket. Arriving at 11 am next Saturday. Are we going to the magical mud volcanoes in Balochistan? Let me know if it's okay with you or not. Else, I will change the bookings. Please, please feel free to speak your mind.

Najam: Sounds good. Not too sure about Balochistan trip. We'll go IF it's safe. I don't have an extra bed arrangement. Hence, it's going to be a couch. Hope it's fine with you. You're coming soon. Wow!

Amy: Safe. Not afraid of dying, it is love that scares me, LOL A couch is fine. Isn't that why it's called *Couchsurfing*? ;)

Najam: I love *Bollywood* too ;) See you at the airport.

***

We'll get along fine, Najam's daydream suggested while he was waiting for her at Arrivals. Short, chubby and strong, Amy resembled one of her two heavy black suitcases. Clad in black tights and matching long-sleeve T-shirt she appeared to be a bit shy in contrast to her social media presence. It was an awkward hug. Najam did most of the talking while driving her to one of his favourite restaurants in town. It was almost lunchtime and was quite a bit of a drive from the airport to his place. Besides she didn't look particularly tired after the long trip.

'Do they have bacon here?' Amy looked excited as she went through the menu of the western-style restaurant.

'I wish. But why would you crave for bacon? You live in America.'

'I can't eat that bacon. It's pork. *Haram*. I was introduced to *halal* beef bacon during my last visit here in Karachi and I hogged it. It's so good!' She laughed for the first time.

'Clearly, you seem to know more about my city than I do.' He was amused. 'It'd be fun ordering some bacon here. Let's ask them.' But there was no bacon for the asking. No pork.

After dropping Amy at his apartment, Najam quickly headed to work. It was a hot and humid Saturday afternoon, a bit more relaxed compared with the weekdays' madness of the news networks. He was hoping not to hear any more news of suicide bombings and mass killings. That was the hardest part of the job.

Later, home after leaving early from work, Najam noticed that Amy had made herself at home straight away in 'the blue room'. He called his guest bedroom the blue room because the walls were painted deep, at times melancholy, blue. The space didn't look as gloomy with her inside as it did when his friends would chain-smoke in there. Najam and Amy went out for dinner to a place called *New York Cafe* where they did serve *halal* bacon. She took some selfies on her phone and smiled broadly while sharing them with her friends. *Well, this is a happy place,* he thought, slumping back in his chair while the vanilla ice cream melted on a piece of hot chocolate cake on the table.

***

The doorbell rang at its usual time in the morning. Najam picked up his phone from the bedside table to check the time. *8 am, always on time*, he thought as he smiled in admiration for the punctuality of his cleaner, Omar. He had entered the apartment with a bundle of news-papers and carefully placed them on the coffee table in the lounge, before he proceeded to raise the blinds. Omar had a short, slim and energetic body and he talked incessantly. He began the cleaning and his spiel almost simultaneously, while Najam skimmed through the newspapers and pretended to listen by occasionally producing 'mm-hmms' from his vocal cords without opening his mouth. He was not interested in the affairs of his neighbours.

'Don't,' Najam said in a sharp voice when Omar grabbed the doorknob of the blue room. He knocked on the door gently. 'Amy, are you up yet?' Nothing. 'Let's not disturb my guest now. We will clean this room tomorrow, alright?'

Omar nodded but, obviously, his inquisitive eyes wanted to know more. As he sipped from his teacup silently, Najam imagined Omar narrating the news of the mysterious 'guest' to a judgmental old woman who lived on the fifth floor.

This was the longest weekend of the year in the country. A four day *Eid* holiday began on Tuesday and most people were expected to go back to work the following Monday. Najam couldn't stand the brazen display of beheadings of so-called 'sacrificial' animals in every street in front of cheering crowds. This was the highlight of Eid in Pakistan – blood everywhere. Fortunately, Amy was not interested in documenting that gross bloodshed. So he planned day trips to some of the mesmerising historical sites in the Interior Sindh.

A couple of other seemingly like-minded couchsurfer types agreed to join them on the excursion. Razzak was a farmer, aged forty-one, who divided his time between Karachi, where he lived with his ageing mother, and a small village in the depths of the prov-ince where he owned a huge expanse of farming land. Razzak was a generous, humble and polite man. Farmers who owned land in Sindh were generally referred to as *wadera* which is a loose translation of a feudal lord. Due to the creation of Pakistan as a nation, this part of what was formerly India never experienced true land reforms. So just a few powerful families owned two-thirds of the farmland across Pakistan. Razzak, despite being a modest and educated man, loved being addressed as a *wadera*.

Their other companion, Khasya, was a very impressionable twenty-four-year-old who was struggling to become some kind of creative content provider. It was hard to work out his ambitions, as they kept changing.

Najam picked up the other two fellow travellers in his silver hatchback Toyota early in the morning, from different parts of the city, before he put the vehicle on the bumpy and narrow National Highway. The trip turned out to be slower than planned, as Amy wanted to jump out of the car with her intimidating gear every time she noticed something interesting to photograph. Nomadic tribes, stray dogs, grazing sheep, dysfunctional public toilets, she kept clicking away. She looked pleased, but it was Khasya who appeared to be massively thrilled by her actions. Eventually, he became her constant assistant and carried her bags throughout. The temperature and the humidity levels rose when the sun moved upwards in the clear sky. They were all wearing thin layers of bright cotton clothes, except for Amy who each day would put on the same black attire. Najam had never seen her in anything besides those many layers she had been wearing on the day of her arrival.

Oh shit! From the car's front seat, Najam nervously looked in the rear view mirror where his eyes met those of Razzak, who was sitting in the back. They'd just got in the car after exploring the historical *Chowkandi Graveyard*. That was when Najam had smelt it the first time, an unbearable odour which hung in the air for the rest of their trip despite the rolling down of windows multiple times. In the communication which Razzak and Najam conducted through their eyes and a few well-placed words, they seemed to agree that the vulgar odour and their discomfort were caused by the presence of a large proportion of polyester in the photographer's outfit, mixed with sweat. Relief came when Khasya offered Amy a motorbike ride back home from Razzak's place where he'd parked his two-wheeler. She readily accepted.

***

Back at the apartment the next day, as soon as Najam opened the lid of his automatic washing machine to chuck some laundry in, he was confronted by the now familiar disgusting smell. As he'd guessed, the black pile of clothes seemed indeed to be Amy's daily uniform.

'Amy, did you forget to pull out your stuff from the washing machine?' he yelled, since the door of the blue room was shut as usual.

'Oh, I am so sorry.' She quickly came out and ran towards the kitchen where the machine was located. 'I forgot.'

Najam looked at her bright pink, polka dot pyjamas and decided he was right about that stinky heap lying in the machine being the only other set of clothes she had. She spread the smelly rags on the drying rack on the balcony.

'Looks like you'll have to wash them again,' he said quietly, trying not to breathe. 'Or maybe I should do it for you.'

Amy didn't hear him.

***

Amy was keen on doing a photo feature on The Foundation's Cradles, probably the country's largest welfare organisation. Among many free and unique services they provided were cradles that were placed outside most of their office buildings, with a sign that read 'Do not kill. Place the child here.' They had been collecting over two hundred and fifty abandoned babies a year. The children were eventually adopted, after a thorough process of screening and background checks of the applicants, supervised by a woman who was referred to as 'the Mother Teresa of Pakistan'. Realising that he had not covered the topic in any of his shows yet, Najam assigned the story to Alia and Ahmed who produced a weekly pre-recorded show dealing with social and human interest issues. He arranged for Amy to go with them so she could take photos of the cradles and the people involved. And as it turned out, she got lucky. Way too lucky.

***

Several hours after the crew set out for filming, Najam's phone rang.
    'What is it, Ahmed?' Najam snapped down the phone.
    'Just this morning someone has left a newborn girl in the cradle.' Ahmed didn't stammer this time.
    'Congratulations. Good for the show. Gotta go ...'
    'Sh ... should we let her adopt the baby?'
    'What? Who?' Najam was annoyed, as he was in the middle of planning that night's prime time live shows.
    'Your friend wants to adopt her. So ... should we ...'
    'Well, she's an adult. She can decide for herself, right? And, what right do we have to prevent that anyway? Please don't call me for these trivial things.' Najam hung up.

***

And so it had come to this, Najam and Amy tense and silent in the car as they returned home from buying essential items for the baby at the supermarket. Once home and after reading the instructions on the baby formula tin, Amy quickly mixed some milk powder with sterilised water in the baby's bottle, shook it, and began feeding the tiny creature in her lap while Najam stood and watched, his shoulders slumped in an attitude of defeat. *He didn't want to say anything about it while it was happening.*
    'Are you upset?' Amy cleared her throat and broke the agonis-

ing silence.

'Yes,' was his almost inaudible reply.

'I'm sorry I didn't tell you. I had been contemplating the concept but I hadn't the faintest idea that I would not only find one but they would then agree to let me adopt her. Look at her. Isn't she an angel?'

He complied and looked at the baby, managing a faint smile. Suddenly a significant story from his childhood burst from his mouth in one long monologue. He couldn't help it. 'It's not that I hate children. I don't. Zevi wanted them and I didn't. We were quite happy together ... except for the times when she'd bring up the question of children, which would freak me out. My reactions caused her hurt and rage. We wouldn't talk for days. I couldn't understand why the notion of becoming a parent was so irrationally frightening to me. I went to a shrink. It was her idea. It didn't fix anything apparently but the therapy helped me find some answers. Zevi left when perhaps for the tenth time I asked her to choose between our marriage and a child. I suppose there was no villain in the story. But it could have been because that little boy who was me tried to keep pace with his selfish speed-walker of a father while it poured raining, and the boy fell in the open sewage. Buried deep in shit, in the midst of laughing adults, he witnessed the figure of his father transforming into a dot. Then he disappeared into nothing.'

Before going to her couch to sleep, Amy told him that she would move to her grandparents' home the next day. Najam went to his room and locked it from the inside.

***

The following night, he was surprised to see her sitting quietly on the couch. He thought she'd be gone by the time he came back from work.

'Where is ... where's the baby?' Najam looked around.

'I can't take her to the US with me.' Amy sounded crushed. 'I don't have the necessary paperwork done. So, I returned her.' She looked into his eyes.

He felt a pang of guilt and looked away. 'How are you feeling?'

'Empty.'

***

Amy left, but not before spending the remainder of the nineteen days on his couch, as she'd planned. They barely spoke. Perhaps they knew they couldn't console one another. She'd bonded with Khasya and he became her shadow. The young man even quit his casual production assistant job to be with her. He practically moved into the blue room for the rest of her days in the city.

Najam pretended to be sleeping on the morning she left. He could hear her suitcases being dragged across the floor and waited anxiously for the sound of the opening and closing of the entrance door. Afterwards, he unlocked his bedroom door and went out to the lounge room to sit on the sofa. He was not sure how he felt. *Is this a relief?* He wondered. In the kitchen to put on the kettle, he saw a 'thank you' card leaning against the blender, with an image of a ripe banana on a bright green background. It read: 'Thank you for the banana milkshakes.'

ROLLER DERBY

JENNIFER NEIL

The roar of the steel wheels on my rollerskates was thunderous. I was trying to beat Myrna Rothwell's record of the night before, roller skating down the highly polished wooden floorboards in our long dormitory.

I was eleven years old and, generally, roller skates in those days were of the most basic design, just four metal wheels on a flat metal base tied on with leather straps. Myrna had the latest thing in roller skates – her skates had plastic wheels which didn't make as much noise. The dormitory I was racing down was about thirty metres long, with twenty beds in straight rows and four rows of beds. So, eighty beds filled with an extremely captive group of spectators cheering me on. At the end of the race, the track went through two doors into a room where the nuns slept. But all the nuns were at their evening prayers, with only a senior prefect in charge and she was chatting away in her dormitory with other senior girls.

I took off from the washroom end, and got a respectable momentum going, waving to my friends as I flew past. A fantastic run! Turning around to go back, I heard a voice bellow out of nowhere, 'Take those skates off now, and come and see me.'

A nun stood there, arms folded, looking as if I had just slapped God in the face. Where did she come from? Where was the girl who was the time-keeper? The girls were having hysterics, laughing at my attempt to break the dormitory record set by Myrna Rothwell.

Oh yes, Myrna Rothwell! She was an amazing, talented sporty girl – my age. She had everything a girl would want: beautiful black wavy hair, long strong legs. In fact, a perfect body. She was always adventurous and brave in all the pursuits we undertook, including crawling under the school fence to walk into town, about two kilometres away, to buy sweets for our midnight feasts.

But there was one thing Myrna Rothwell could not do, she could not swim. So she didn't compete in the swimming carnivals. When, after hockey practice one day, Myrna told our hockey coach she couldn't swim, Miss Hersh immediately offered to teach her to swim, just two weeks before the carnival.

Oh yes! Miss Hockey Sticks had taught me to dive off the high board, and was a very touchy-feely woman. I had won the 50 metres over the previous two years, with my sister, Ann, coming second. On carnival day, as we took off I noticed Myrna jump in. *Lucky me, she can't dive*, I thought, expecting now that she also wouldn't be able to swim fast, after only two weeks of training.

Well, Myrna Rothwell went streaking past me so fast I nearly stopped swimming to have a look. She came first and I came second, with Ann third. I really hated Myrna for that. She was completely cool about her win, just another arrow added to her quiver. She didn't have to be so damned nonchalant about it all. Pity she was my best friend; I had to give in gracefully.

Anyway, back at the roller derby, I was going pretty fast in the race and the shock of seeing Sister Dolma meant I nearly fell down the stairs, trying to miss her as I stopped. I took the skates off and gave them to the angry nun. Then she screamed at me, 'You will kneel out every night for two weeks.'

'Just two weeks?' I asked sarcastically. Whereupon, she ran towards me with her arm raised, ready to hit me. I should point out that I had the running record for the dormitory race, and had taken off before she'd moved an inch.

Kneeling out involved kneeling on the bare floor boards of the dormitory for an hour each night. It was a painfully tedious experience. There was no talking to your friends; only senior prefects could talk to you. Most of my friends came past and 'side-talked' me. This was managed by walking slowly past a person and talking out the side of the mouth. Myrna, who was, after all, my best friend, was side talking with her back to the nun's room, when a nun's voice bellowed at her to kneel out as well. What happiness! We side-talked to each other all night.

On the second monotonous night of the two-week stint, a senior girl called Jean Anderson, stopped in front of me, and posed a question: 'Do you know what a lesbian is?'

'No,' I said. 'What is that?'

'It's when two women make love,' she said, and calmly walked off.

I was beside myself with this exhilarating information. I knew something my peer group did not know. That night after lights out, I crawled along the dorm to all my friends' beds, to tell them what Jean Anderson had told me. Of course, Myrna Rothwell said she already knew what a lesbian was, her mother was one.

'No, Myrna, she can't be,' I said.

'Yes, she is,' said Myrna. 'Her girlfriend comes and stays when my father goes away on business.' God, Myrna always knew everything!

Years later, my kids used to tell their friends their mother was a lesbian. In fact, I know my daughter, Susan, used to want to shock her friends with this information about me. I have to say, the things I learned while 'kneeling out' have lasted me a lifetime.

AUNTIE ANNIE'S JUBILEE

JIM PIOTROWSKI

It's a private matter, one's faith. Or that's what *they* say, but I want to share a story, which I'm not sure if I shouldn't be ashamed of, but I feel an obligation to convey.

I do not believe that Jesus Christ died for my sins, that Allah cares in any way what I do, or that saying God's name hurts his feelings. I came to this belief through want of a belief that I could believe. I didn't think that was too much to ask of a belief, but apparently it is.

You gotta have faith.

My Auntie Annie must have faith because she's been a Catholic nun for seventy years.

Auntie Annie is a relative on Mum's side, her older cousin, which makes her a 'cousin-once-removed' to me, rather than an auntie, but 'Auntie' is what we call her.

I don't know Auntie Annie that well, but I love her. Mum said that she had been known to be a little wild before she took her vows. And she has always had a bit of a glint in her eyes, though these days it's more of a stare. She follows the footy and goes for Wests Tigers, which is my team, so that's a connection. She privately agreed with me once that the church should change its celibacy rule and allow priests to marry. At family events we are openly agnostic and she doesn't seem to mind at all. She has a beer. She's quite conservative, I think. Well, compared to us. I wonder if she believes. I hope she does. I don't like to ask.

We were brought up as cultural Catholics. Our parents didn't 'believe in the church' but they had us baptised and sent us to a Catholic school because they thought that was the right thing to do. The good thing about a Catholic upbringing is that it gives you a healthy cynicism of Catholicism. It's a very cynical religion. Do as I say, not as I do. Happily hypocritical, that's our culture.

So regardless of our beliefs, I think we've always been a little proud to have a 'Sister' in our clan.

Sister Anne is ninety-one and has been a Catholic nun since the age of twenty-one. My mother, sister and I went to her Jubilee at the Catholic Nursing Home for Retired Nuns where she lives. The Jubilee was a celebration for three women with holy service between sixty-five and seventy-five years duration. The afternoon involved a full Catholic Mass in the humble chapel and an afternoon tea in the tidy function room.

On the way there I had in my mind an idea, a test of my own beliefs that involved a Catholic Mass. And my idea would fit well with my intention, as a mark of respect to Sister Anne, to participate fully in the mystical pagan ritual, which is the Catholic Mass.

That's what you do when you're brought up a Catholic; even if you don't believe, you go through the motions, recite rote responses to the psalms, mumble along with the songs.

We were seated in the second row of pews, in the front of the church, right in the priest's eyeline. I endeavoured to look as a believer might look.

It had been a while since I'd tried to fake it in a mass, so the songs were all different to what I remembered, and the tunes were awkward to sing along with. Even with the commemorative Jubilee booklet, the songs all seemed repetitive without any sense of metre or rhyme, and the congregational responses had been varied or I'd just forgotten them. It was like that.

But the sermon was easy. I couldn't remember the last time I'd heard a sermon. And it was a good one, I thought, simple and delivered with sincere eyes and an open heart, so I almost forgave the elderly priest for selectively misquoting the good book.

'God has only one question to ask anyone,' he said, 'and that question is – regardless of what might be said elsewhere – the only question God wants us to answer is, "Will you let me love you?"'

I thought he said it as if it was an apology for all the other things the Bible says. He seemed a smart enough type of guy.

No problem, I answered in my head. *Give me all your loving, it's all welcome here.*

There's no way he believes, I thought, *and if he does, he's embarrassed by his faith.*

And I was wondering, *Do Christians believe in the Old Testa-*

ment? Do we have to kill the Canaanites as well?

As I said, I went to a Catholic school but I wasn't the brightest student. I was average, so maybe some genius understood the teachings better than I did, but Yahweh says, among other things, to kill the Canaanites and all of their descendants.

Like, why would I want to go back in time and immerse myself in a geopolitical shit storm, and hate a whole race of people that I know nothing about? That's what the Bible says I should do. Or not. Jesus brought a new and everlasting covenant, as if the old agreement wasn't everlasting, as if you didn't really need to be circumcised to show that you were a believer. But they sing songs to Yahweh in the Catholic Mass. What's that all about? Do we have 10 Commandments or 613? There are 613 Commandments in the Jewish Bible, which is basically the Christian Old Testament, so what's going on with these testaments and covenants and commandments? All of these deals that God made that may no longer apply if you haven't been genitally mutilated. But what if you have been? Is that good or bad? I don't know. You read the word of God and it doesn't make sense. God is so full of contradictions I don't know what he's going on about. So maybe no one does.

Throughout the service I was thinking about my plan: a way out of this pagan birth rite, so I didn't have to recite things that made no sense, sings songs that had no rhythm, endorse genocide.

The Lamb of God takes away the sins of the world. What on Earth does that mean? It means that the Eucharist is coming!

You see for some time I'd had the notion of excommunication on my mind. It seemed the honourable thing to do, to quit the club I'd never asked to join. But there are so many cultural details that act as impediments, like my Mum. And atheism is such a strong word. Are you an atheist if you believe in the universe? I mean as far as I know the universe exists, but should it be worshipped?

I don't think it's necessary.

I told a friend, a cultural Catholic I grew up with, that I wanted to get excommunicated. He said that I didn't need to do anything.

'Just keep doing what you're doing,' he said, 'and when the day of reckoning comes your name won't be on the list.' He was very matter of fact with this advice, but still I felt that some specific action was required.

I don't think the Pope accepts unsolicited correspondence and I didn't want to write to the local Catholic priest and advise him that I was an apostate. I didn't want to hurt his feelings. I had no idea who the local priest was but I didn't want to ruin his day, make him feel responsible for the errors of his faith. Worse still, I was sure he wouldn't really be a believer either, so it would be like rubbing salt into his wounds.

I googled, *How to get excommunicated*, looking for options. From the lists that emerged, it seemed to me that the most practical way was to desecrate a consecrated host. It's a mortal sin and results in automatic excommunication, directly from God, as I understand it.

So I was sitting in the church at Auntie Annie's Jubilee and the priest told me that all God wanted was to let him love me and I let him love me and that was all fine. But I wanted more from the service. I wasn't sure if I'd ever have the opportunity again. I watched the priest and considered the best approach to take as the congregation of elderly nuns and their relatives lined up to take Holy Communion.

I imagined taking the host, throwing it at my feet and stomping on it, right in front of the priest. But that wouldn't do. It would upset him and Auntie Annie and Mum and all the little sisters of the poor. I just couldn't do it.

But I had to seize the opportunity and get hold of the body of Christ. There was a gap in the line and I jumped up. It came to my turn and the priest put the host in my cupped hands and he said something like, 'Body of Christ,' and as I walked away, like a gutless heretic, I pretended to put the blessed sacrament in my mouth, but put my hands down religiously and slipped the host in my pocket, with my house keys.

Excommunication occurred at that moment. I can report that from a personal perspective, heresy is no different from Catholicism.

After Mass ended, the congregation applauded the three Jubilarians as they led the procession out of the chapel with their support people. Mum is blind with macular degeneration and well into her eighties and somehow got mixed in among the principal people moving out. My sister pointed out that it looked like the Mass was lauding Mum. And we both enjoyed a laugh at her expense, though she laughed too when we told her later.

Everyone proceeded through an adjoining hall, zimmer frames all over the place, making our way to the function room, where there had to be some careful table management. I think the room was usually their dining room, but they opened some doors to accommodate the crowd of a hundred or so.

The air was all tea cosies and unrequited love. The nuns were old and there were no new girls coming through. It was the end of an era, the end of a religion, I thought, growing old through afternoon tea, waiting for eternal life.

Our friendly cousin, Laura, and her devout husband, Paul, were at the table with us. There was also some middle-class Catholic-type woman who was a school principal, I think, and Sister Josephine, a wild-haired woman in her eighties, who had been assigned to our table. In that crowd I couldn't talk to Mum or my sister about my excommunication and was hoping they wouldn't joke about my 'taking Communion'. They hadn't participated in the Eucharist. We didn't do that in our family, so I expected them to mention it.

'What are you doing, taking Communion?' my sister said, laughing, making Mum giggle too.

'Well, I was just being civilised and paying a bit of respect for Sister Anne, if you don't mind,' I said. 'I thought the sermon was quite nice,' I added, in an effort to change the topic – and everyone agreed they were happy to let God love them.

I spoke with Auntie Annie briefly in the chapel and at the function. Both times she held my hand too long. I let her, but wondered what I should do. So I just held her hand and congratulated her on her achievement. We weren't on her main table so now the closer relatives and their baby granddaughter seemed to take most of her attention. She seemed happy.

I was seated next to Sister Josephine, who advised me that she and Sister Anne were old mates. They watched the footy together on Sunday afternoons. We worked out that she grew up in the same area as me, which made her a Wests Tigers supporter too and that was good enough to gain my confidence. We agreed it would take a miracle for the Tigers to get into the finals. She had a cheeky way about her. I wasn't sure if it was caused by senility, but we had a friendly chat. She asked me three times where I lived. I told her twice, but the third time I turned the question around and asked her where she thought I might live. And she knew the answer! I don't think she got to talk with outsiders very often.

'Can God forgive a mortal sin?' I asked her.

'Of course!' she said, and tapped the table with her fingertips, a wicked look in her eyes.

It was all very friendly, nibbling on tiny sandwiches, sipping on tea, everyone was nice to each other. It was such a pleasant occasion, so full of goodwill that I was glad I hadn't made a public event of losing my religion. It was a private matter, after all.

AN EMASCULATING LANDSCAPE

JODY HARPER

Standing on the front verandah of his country homestead, Stan stared blankly towards the glowing sunset, leaning back slightly against the verandah, cold beer in hand, deep in thought. Maxie sat by his feet, his black and white coat covered in a layer of red dust. The shearers had gone home early that day.

Not enough work.

The familiar echo in his mind chimed in. Another day without rain. Another day of failure. The surrounding land was dry and arid. Hardened, deeply dehydrated, cracking at the seams, with splints and shards of defeat evident everywhere he looked across his property. Staring back at him were lifeless fields of despair, lonely and desperate for respite. It was their sixth year of drought.

Treywomble was a small farming community in far western New South Wales, south west of Dubbo. The nearest town was forty minutes away, where 'The Rabbit Hole' local pub and a basic store were located. The town population was around seven hundred, so everyone knew everyone. Stan had been one of the largest sheep breeders in the district, known for his smart business acumen, with fair pay to his workers and sharp instincts.

Stan was third generation Harrington. The family property 'Yidaki', had been passed down from his late father, Mitch Harrington. Stan began shearing from the age of six, during his school holidays waking up with his father and the workers every day at 5 am. Over the years, he'd formed a strong friendship with Daku, a traditional indigenous Australian boy who was three years older than him. Now a man, Daku was still one of the property's best workers, and Stan's closest mate.

As he stood on his verandah, Stan reminisced about his late father, Mitch. He recalled in his childhood when his father would take the ute into town for supplies. Windows down, fresh air blowing through Stan's hair, the freedom of the open road, their cattle dog, Bronte, beside him, wagging his furry tail and licking his face. 'Happy as a pig in shit,' his Dad would say. Stan would beg his father to skip returning him to boarding school once the holidays were over. His father finally relented when Stan turned sixteen. Mitch had known it was time for his boy to become a man.

Stan's grandfather, Robert Harrington, had moved to country New South Wales from Sydney, seeking a simple life. He'd bought the Yidaki station with 'the last pennies in his pocket,' making a handsome living from his investment. His favourite pastime was sitting with his wife, Jean, on this same verandah, watching the sunset and listening to the sound of nothing. As the sun set and the blistering hues of the radiant night sky began to fade, he would play a gentle tune on his harmonica. Jean would take to her crochet, with a small smile and rosy cheeks, slowly swaying in her yellow rocking chair, and adjusting the kerosene lamp for more light as it grew darker.

Stan was prone to the same custom with his love, Janice. They'd been married for near thirty years, and had raised two sons together. Stan had known since Marcus was a toddler that he would become a farmer. Sam, on the other hand, sought out life in the city after his time in boarding school, and was keen to build on his skills in school football to pursue a career in professional rugby union.

The boys were close but didn't speak that often. Sam would come back home for Easter and Christmas, sometimes in between. Father and son would always embrace with a warm hug, Stan ruffling Sam's hair as he saw the reality of his boy now being a man. The two brothers would exchange pleasantries and always greet their Mum with a kiss on the cheek and a tight embrace.

Now, here on the verandah, Janice's sweet voice broke Stan's train of thought.

'Honey, dinner is ready. Come on in and get washed up. Marcus won't be here tonight. He's staying over at Cheryl's.'

Stan took a last swig of his beer and murmured, 'Okay, darl, on my way.' He already knew where Marcus was. He'd planned it that way.

Old Maxie moved with him, right on his heels as he opened the door to go inside. Stan reached down and patted Maxie on the head,

'Thatta boy, we'll see you after dinner.' Obedient, Maxie took his spot at the front door, paw resting over paw as he got comfortable. 'Good dog,' Stan said as he ventured inside.

'What's for dinner, love?' he asked politely as he headed for their bedroom, pulling his flannel shirt off and unlacing his dirty boots. *No more being in trouble for that one*, he thought. Janice reminded him daily about leaving his dirty boots at the front door.

'Baked dinner, love. And the "taters" are crispy, just how you like them.'

Stan stood at the basin and flicked a splash of water across his face. Despair stared back at him, igniting his immense feeling of resignation. Every day it had become harder. He felt completely desperate that he couldn't tell a soul.

What would people think of him?

Remnants of water landed on the bathroom mirror. *Something else I'll be in the shit about*, he thought idly. Looking at his reflection in the mirror, eyes dark and shadowed with strain, he noticed the increasing grey in his hair, camouflaged by a long finger smear on the glass left behind from the recent dust storm. *A baked dinner, eh? How can we afford that luxury?* were his immediate thoughts. *We've got no money left.*

***

It was 6:30 pm. Showered, he entered the dining room, noticing the candle burning and the special occasion crockery on the table. A panic rose in him. Had he forgotten a birthday, anniversary, something special? Had he not timed everything perfectly?

'What's the occasion, love? You've got all the fancy stuff out,' he said, as he kissed Janice on the forehead after she'd wandered in with the gravy boat.

'Sit down,' she said. 'It'll get cold quick'. He took his place at the head of the table, and she prepared his plate. Janice was an excellent cook.

'How was today? I noticed the boys went home early,' she ventured, holding a glass of red wine in her right hand. She took a small sip.

Stan knew she was being tactful. But how long could he hide the truth? He didn't want to worry her. He didn't want her to go without. It was his job to provide. He knew she'd been making all kinds of sacrifices. She was selfless and loyal. A proud woman, she never complained. Not once. He didn't want to let her down, let her know he couldn't go on.

I'm not the man she deserves, he thought.

More dark thoughts swirled in his mind, as he put down his knife and fork, and wiped his mouth with the white linen napkin.

'Neacie, love. We need to talk. I need to tell you ...' He stopped mid-sentence; she was already up and beside him, arms wrapped around his shoulders.

'I know, I know. You don't have to say. I know,' she said as she kissed the top of his head. 'It's okay'.

A feeling of complete failure overwhelmed him. Years of tradition in his bones, years of hard work passed on from his grandfather. The family name, his heirloom. He couldn't go on. He had nothing left. *No, she didn't know*, he thought.

'I'm beat, Neacie, I can't see a way to go on. We can't pay wages this month.'

'Stan, honey, I've picked up a catering job. I know it's not want you want. But I've done the maths and with the little extra coming in we can make it work. I can make it work. We're in this together.'

Stan looked up at his beautiful wife, staring down at him, the purity of her love reaching into his every pore. His eyes welled with tears, his chin quivered as he bent his head down.

'I can't do go on like this, Neacie,' he murmured, more to himself than her.

His broad shoulders began to shake, and he held his head in his hands as he began to sob. She didn't deserve this. He'd checked their life insurance – it was sitting on his bedside table. *She'll be okay*, he thought.

'I'm sorry, Neacie, I'm sorry. I'm sorry it's come to this.'

Janice didn't say a word, just held her husband tightly and let him release. She was petrified for her husband; she'd never seem him like this before.

Eventually, after much cajoling it seemed, the night slowly resumed its normality. They finished their meal and completed their nightly chores. Janice assumed they might have a sherry out on the verandah together.

Stan turned to her, 'I'm going to sit outside with Maxie for a bit, if you don't mind, love. I'll see you upstairs.' Slightly offended, she turned to the grandfather chair for her craft pattern before she touched his arm and kissed the top of his head. 'Okay then. See you upstairs, Stan-boy.'

The old woolshed at Yidaki held many memories for Stan. Special times with his dad, his grandfather, bustling about with his brother James, even private moments with Neacie. It was built high, solid and was currently empty, with no burring of animals in these hard times. He sat and waited until the lamp in their upstairs room had gone out.

A banging on the door early the next morning woke Janice suddenly. She reached for Stan. Where was he? Where was Stan? No sign of him. His hat was still on the dressing table, keys on the sideboard. She noticed a large envelope sitting on his bedside table. Reaching for her dressing gown, she raced downstairs, to see Maxie running up and down the verandah, frantic and barking furiously.

What was Daku bashing on the door for?

'Janice, Janice,' his words screamed through the door before she'd opened the wooden frame. 'It's Stan, Miss. I'm sorry, Miss, I couldn't …' He hesitated to explain further, in dread of speaking the truth, straining to hide the horrified expression on his face.

Immediately she knew. She felt it right away. Her Stan. Her rock. Her everything. Her tower of strength.

Daku caught her as she fell, her head narrowly missing the thud of the hard verandah floor. 'I'm sorry, Miss. I came here as soon as I saw. I'm sorry, I couldn't …' His voice faltered again. Maxie nudged him, demanding an explanation.

Janice couldn't speak. Her throat dried up, her eyes blurred with the enormity of her realisation.

Daku held her in his lap, repeating the same words over and over, 'I'm so sorry, I'm sorry, Miss.'

Maxie continued yelping, his thick frame racing back and forth again and again, up and down the verandah, seeking his master. Daku clicked his fingers at him. 'Maxie, boy. Come here, boy.'

Inside Maxie's collar was a note, folded carefully so it wouldn't fall out. Daku hesitated to touch it. Janice had seen it too and shakily guided his hand to the neatly folder paper.

'Read it, Daku. Her voice, barely a whisper, pleaded, 'Please, for me …'

Daku took the note and held it in his hand, shame that he couldn't read and write engulfing him. In that moment, it was what Miss needed most from him but he couldn't give it to her.

Gingerly, he opened the note, took her hand and closed his eyes. His memory of his last English lesson at school haunted him. The others in the class, all white-skinned, laughing at him when he couldn't pronounce the words. He'd stared blankly at the faces mocking him, seeking a safe place to hide his shame.

Then, he had frozen – but he wouldn't freeze now, not for Miss.

He knew what the note was about, and he knew Stan was a proud and humble man. Lying on the verandah, Janice's body was soft and limp but her bony hand clenched his forearm.

'Miss …' he ventured carefully, taking a deep breath and holding her protectively. 'The note says …' and he told her what needed to be said.

FOURTEEN TWO. ENCOUNTER

Sam Herzog

Charles had the presence of a local schizophrenic in a small town –
strong and invasive.

It was 9 pm when he flew through the entrance like a jumbo jet,
touching down on the seat next to me. The bar's atmosphere suddenly
shifted, as if Ted Bundy had just stumbled into a tender tween's slum-
ber party. The six couples spread sparely across the venue all gave
Charles a look. I tried not to.

Charles was agitated, his firecracker limbs reacting violently to
every minor stimulus. The bartender asked him if he wanted a drink.
'Yes, yes!' he said. 'A Guinness!' He was dressed somewhat shabbily,
though he wasn't without some style: a stained tweed jacket wrapped
tightly around a stout, shuffling physique.

The attention on Charles was finally broken when the trivia
host declared the next round of questions. For the last fifteen minutes, she'd been sitting on a stool in the corner, slowly accumulating
the required motivation to continue. Now, she slid from her seat and
sauntered over to the bar. She ordered a Red Bull with vodka. As the
bartender poured her the drink, she offered the words *Rooound Threee*
to the microphone in a kind of saline drawl.

The couples went back to playing their game. I looked upon
them with jealousy; it was Valentine's Day and I was alone. Me alone
with my schooner of sadness. Those times feel so different when I
look back on them. Now I have a wife and a wonderful family and the
colours of cynicism that painted my younger years have undoubtedly
faded (though perhaps my wife would disagree with this).

It was raining outside and windy. The wild weather hounded

passers-by on the street. Charles wiped the wet from his hands onto his trousers. He took a sip of Guinness. I stole another glance at him. He seemed to have calmed, the alcohol having unstrung some of the tension in his limbs. At that moment, Charles struck me as someone who might have no qualms about striking up a conversation with a stranger. Just in case, I used my body language to arrest any attempt at conversation.

But my change in orientation had no effect. He started a conversation with me anyway.

'Jesus. Fucking wild out there tonight, no?' he said, tapping me on the shoulder. I felt the big wide eyes burn a hole through the back of my head.

'Mm,' I replied. I did not turn around.

'What's your name, eh?' he said. It was now impossible not to turn around.

'I-I'm William.'

'Charles,' he said, almost without a beat, holding out a hand. I shook it.

'Long day, Willy boy. Long, long day.'

'Oh yeah?' I said, kicking myself internally. I realised how my false enthusiasm was now going to prolong the conversation.

He began to describe how he'd just broken up with 'a beautiful spectacular girl'. 'Beautiful like a prime Atlantic codfish, she was! But I had to end it. I'm completely insufferable. Oh, woe is me!' he wailed. 'Why am I the way I am – cursed with this intolerably neurotic disposition?'

I noticed how he spoke in a kind of rolling grandiose manner.

'William. Will,' he said, patting me on the shoulder. 'You know, I heard an expression once: "Everywhere you go, there you are right there with you." Fuck: that's it, Willy, that's the ticket, that is. What I'd *give* to get away from myself for even just a spoonful of time.'

I looked up at the bartender who was cleaning a glass in front of us. We made eye contact in the way where you can tell you're both thinking the same thing.

'Well, what happened?'

'What happened? Well, I'm just a fucking crazy, is what happened. None of it makes any sense, William. Nothing. Nada!' Charles yelled, accidently swiping a jar of cutlery which crashed onto the floor beside us. A couple busy playing trivia nearby turned and glared at us. I also spotted some of Charles' spit which had flown from his mouth and settled on the rim of my glass. He noticed all this and tried to calm himself.

'William, I want to tell you this story, okay? I don't know how long it's going to go on for, but I need you to listen to it all the way through. If I get interrupted or have to stop at any point for any reason, I'll go absolutely mad and there'll have been no point in me telling you. So, don't interrupt, okay?'

I opened my mouth to speak but Charles interrupted me, launching into his narrative.

'My full name is Charles James Stuart. I was born in the UK, but my parents were from a small town in Slovenia. The name of the town was *Bled*. You know, like, "I touched my aunt Edith with a pencil and she *Bled*" – he, he!'

Charles' asides were accompanied by a rapid flicking gesture he made with his hands. 'My mother and my father left that place and moved to the East End of London. After I was born, at some point I came here. I am currently forty-eight years and seven months old. My favourite colour is red.'

'Okay …'

'Anyway, three months ago I met a girl. A beautiful spectacular girl – spectacular like a top-tier European salmon I would say! Her name was Abbey. Abbey was beautiful. She was so absolutely stunning that I don't think I could ever meet a girl like that again. She had strawberry blonde hair and a beautiful slender face, and this wonderful, beautiful figure. Her background was some sort of Spanish-Chinese-French-Italian-something. (Hence her beauty, you know!)'

I attempted to probe the bartender's reaction, but he'd gone out the back. Now it was just me and Charles.

'I met her three months ago. I was in the supermarket buying a loaf of bread. Was it bread or was it milk? Bread. It was bread. I know it was because I wanted to make a sandwich and I didn't have any bread. So I went to go buy some, you see?'

I nodded.

'Anyway, I'm in the bread aisle and I see this loaf of bread in front of me. I think to myself: "Now, my oh my, this is a beautiful and spectacular loaf of bread, this is." So, I go to pick it up, and right as I go, another hand reaches for the same loaf of bread. There was only one of these loaves left, you see, so that's why we both went for the same loaf of bread.'

'And so Abbey went for the same loaf and that's how you met,' I said.

Charles' eyes narrowed. 'No … No, it was my mother. I ran into my mother in the supermarket. I met Abbey at the checkout – she was working at the checkout – and I met my mother in the bread aisle. We went for the same loaf of bread. … Where was I? Fuck, I can't remember now.' Charles looked like he'd been pushed over by a stranger while trying to tie his shoelaces in the street. 'I told you not to interrupt, William,' he said with venom.

I quickly apologised and urged him to continue.

'Anyway … so I spoke to my mother … and then … said I had to go. I had to go make this sandwich. I was fucking hungry!' Charles spread his arms wide. 'So, I pissed off from Mum and headed to the checkout. … Aha! And this is where I met Abbey.'

Charles' face suddenly lit up with a soft delight.

'And there she was, standing there, thin girl that she is. Beautiful. She's standing there with her beautiful red hair and pale skin. Glowing almost, her skin is. Anyway, I'm putting my bread through and I notice this. This glowing. She's standing by the self-serve, maybe four or three or two-and-a-half metres away, and I say "Abbey" (I knew her name because it was written on her name badge). I say "Abbey", and she comes over and I tell her. I tell her about her glowing skin. I say "Abbey, you're absolutely beautiful and I love you. You've got a wonderful soul, you have. I haven't even met you and I just know it." Anyway, she was naturally flattered and so I said, "Abbey, please, will you come out to dinner with me tomorrow night? I want to take you out to dinner," and she said, "Yes, okay then," and so we went.

'We go out to dinner and that's that. Just like that, you know, we're on. She's perfect – funny, sexy, good in the book department – she works in a book department – and we get on great. And anyway, all of this is good until a little while later, maybe a few weeks. Something … happens …'

Charles suddenly seemed disturbed. He became timorous like a frightened kitten. The bartender returned from out the back and resumed listening.

'We're sitting at this restaurant,' continued Charles. 'Thai food or something. … No. Mexican. *Raoul's Mexicana*. Nice place but the sauce is too hot. Anyway, we're sitting there – eating. And I'm looking down at my food and I'm saying, "Abbey, isn't the sauce too hot here?" and I look at her and she's looking down at her food, assaulting a piece of guacamole with a fork. And suddenly it hits me. This awful, awful, dreadful thought! Oh, God, it's too much to bear. I can't bear it,' he groaned.

Charles paused.

The bartender and I held our breaths in anticipation.

'A-And this thought … it lingers, you know? I just can't rid myself of it. It's there and it doesn't go away. And we continue to eat and there it is; it's just sitting there with us,' Charles said, squirming.

'What was the thought?' I asked. I immediately anticipated a reproach, but Charles didn't say anything. Instead, he looked down at his beer, aghast.

'Well, what was it?' the bartender asked.

'She doesn't say much!' Charles suddenly blurted out.

'What?'

'That she doesn't talk enough,' he repeated.

The bartender and I stared at him blankly. Charles sensed he needed to elaborate.

'I'll give you an example. Not long ago, we went and saw a film. An Owen Wilson film. Normally, I don't see his films because he's a bit of a, you know …' Charles made a strange hand gesture that I didn't know how to interpret. 'But anyway, we go. We see the film. It's good. Not a bad film, actually. A very nuanced performance of a man who doesn't know the difference between left and right and the associated struggles of such a disposition.'

Charles took a sip of Guinness.

'As we're leaving the cinema, Abbey says, "What did you think about Owen Wilson?" Now, this is a very specific question and so I give her a very specific answer. I say, "Darling, I thought it was a very nuanced performance of a man who doesn't know the difference between left and right and his struggles with such a disposition." But I go into more detail, you know: "Oh, the scene where he's in the car and the sign says *No Right Turn* and he doesn't know what to do and the cars behind are honking at him … Just tragic … Or when Owen Wilson's grandfather dies and he can't find the funeral home. The man with the terrier says: *You take two left turns and then a right.* Then Wilson ends up at the White House! … How fucking lachrymose."'

Charles frowned.

'Then I say, "What about you darling, what did you think?" And you know what she says?'

He paused.

'She says, "It was good."'

I gave Charles a blank look, not knowing how I was supposed to react. He quickly averted his gaze and faced the front of the bar, silent. He took an anguished sip of beer.

'I couldn't stop thinking about that comment for two whole weeks,' he said, still facing forward. 'She's wonderful, wonderful, that girl. Love everything about her. *But can I really be with someone who is destitute of opinion?* I keep thinking to myself. When we're together, it's all I can think about!'

He took a deep breath. 'So, I decided I couldn't take it anymore, you know? This … doubt, I had to end it.'

'So, you broke up with her?' the bartender interrupted. I expected a reproach, but Charles was calm.

'No. ... No, I didn't break up with her. I loved her too much. I came home one night after work and I sat down on the couch and I planned out my ... response.'

'So, what did you do?' I asked.

Charles flashed a look of irritation. 'Willy, what did I say about interrupting? I'm getting to that.' He stared down at his beer for a long moment.

Then he looked up, as if awakening from a deep reverie. 'Do you know why we tell stories?' he asked.

'Entertainment?' I said.

'No. Yes, but no. Evolution, my friend. Evolution. Or morality rather. It's all about morality. Cause and effect. We tell stories because they're all about how to act. They're information. Stories are interesting because hidden in them are directions, messages, for how to act in the world.'

'Right.'

'Think about it: the structure of nearly every story is conflict and resolution. All stories must have a conflict, otherwise what you have is a ... a documentary. Stories must have a conflict because they must present a problem to the audience. A problem that the audience might find themselves in. But that's not all; a story must have a resolution. How the problem is solved. What did the characters do and what results did this lead to? Maybe Owen Wilson decided that, even though he didn't know the difference between left and right, he would take the job as the Washington city planner. And then he goes and builds a daycare centre right next to the bloody airport; all the little buggers end up having to learn sign language! This whole scenario is interesting because we can see the cause and effect – which of Wilson's actions led to what results. Thus, if we find ourselves in a similar situation, we know how to act – or how not to act. Now, of course, if there's something I wanted you to do, or some important lesson I wanted to teach you, I could just tell you how you should act. I could just say, "William, my boy, if you don't know the difference between left and right then you'd bloody better not dabble your Dylan in the town planning profession!" But: you know what the problem with that is? You wouldn't listen! We don't listen to each other's advice. It's not in our nature. But if I tell you a story, Willy, a story about Owen Wilson deafening some small children ... Well, in that case – he, he!'

Charles began scratching his face with a talon. I struggled to see how this diatribe was related to his conundrum with Abbey. The bartender was also confused. Charles went on.

'I couldn't tell Abbey about this dissatisfaction of mine. I couldn't do it. She was a sensitive girl, you know, always getting upset about animals getting run over or something. I didn't want to hurt her, eh? But I couldn't hold my silence either.'

'And?'

'And so I began to write a fucking story, boys, keep up! I used my imagination to engineer a cunning narrative to implicitly tell Abbey my dissatisfactions without actually telling her, you see? At the heart of the story would be my central message! I started to research – newspaper clippings, discourses with the postman, *Wikipedia*. I'm a perfectionist, you see. If I was going to do this, I had to do a good job of it; otherwise, I would be stuck in my current situation and that wasn't going to be favourable to anyone. So, I thought out this story.' Charles revealed a flash of hubris. 'This is how it goes.

'There's a girl named Carrie Carlyle who lives in a one-bedroom studio apartment all by herself. She works for a film distribution company and her role is essentially to market films to the cinemas. Though she is relatively happy and lives a contented life, she senses a pernicious protrusion somewhere in her steamrolled-smooth existence. But she can never quite figure out what it is. Her cat's name is Snozzlebert Cumbercooch.'

' …'

'Anyway, one day a man comes into her office. His name is Anthony Kovacs, a Hungarian-by-heritage, self-made millionaire who owns a successful cinema chain. Due to declining company profits, Kovacs has decided to take a break from his current life beguiling handmaidens with salacious poetry. This is in order to take a more active role in the company and bring it back to its former glory. Mr Kovacs decides that he's going to take on the executive decisions of which films to purchase and distribute that season. The trouble is Kovacs is a literary kind of man. He's into poetry – books, words, that sort of thing. But he's only ever seen just nine or seven films in his entire life! He's not into the visual aesthetic other than when it comes to the opposite sex. Thus, in order to decide which films to purchase, he pays a visit to Carrie Carlyle's open-plan office.

'Now, Carrie is sitting at her desk like any other day, distractedly scrolling through photos of Snozzlebert Cumbercooch, when who should enter but "Oh, Mr Kovacs". Naturally, everyone in the office is blown away – they've all read about Kovacs in the newspapers – about the adventures and scandals that he's been wrapped up in. Such as the time Kovacs flew a little two-seater Bonanza over the Eiffel Tower (backwards) in order to impress the French president's missus. Or the "Singleton Affair", as the papers called it – the time Kovacs made a mission over to Palestine in order to retrieve a radioactive dictionary that the Palestinians had been using to irradiate Israeli goats.

'So, anyway, everyone in the office is naturally fawning over this Mr Kovacs. But suddenly, who should catch his fine, dark, Hungarian eye? Miss Carrie Carlyle. Kovacs flitters over to our heroine protagonist and starts secreting his usual charm all over her. Miss Carlyle is normally resistant to such secretions, and she is familiar with Kovacs' reputation. So, she isn't going to give up the goods easily, "even if he is a millionaire" or "even if it is a Friday afternoon", as one of Carrie's fellow colleagues points out. "Never, no way, I don't care how poetical this oleaginous gentleman might be," says Carrie to the co-worker.

'Though Kovacs' thoughts are now on a different sort of business, he does start to question Miss Carlyle about the available films for purchase – his original mission. And she of course gives him the spiel about the films. Although Kovacs knows nothing of them, one of them catches his attention, a certain little nothing about an old woman who is concerned with the height of her hedge. Kovacs asks Carrie if she has seen this film and she has. Now this is the important part we are coming to, so pay attention.

'Kovacs noticed this particular film because the main character is played by an American actor with whom he is vaguely familiar. "So, what is it like, Owen Wilson's performance? I know him," says Kovacs. "What I've heard is that he is able to wiggle his ears along in a certain rhythmic pulsation. He wiggles along at an increased rate, in synchrony with the underlying dramatic tension of the film, so that by the time the climax arrives, we are so wound up that we are forced to feel its full release at one hundred times the original intensity!" Carrie Carlyle gives him a blank look. "So, did you feel this about his acting or was I mistaken?" asks Kovacs. Carrie Carlyle looks him straight in the eyes and tells him – get this – that she thought, "It was good" – with no further elaboration.

'Kovacs is satisfied and immediately purchases the rights to the film. But, oh, woe! If he had just heard a little more about the specifics of the performance! (Oh, God, my goodness.) If only Carrie had not merely contained her commentary to "It was good" and given her real opinion instead, then Mr Kovacs would have been more sceptical and not invested so heavily in the film. What happened is that Kovacs went away and lost a ton of money on this cinematic squalor. And then, because he was annoyed and fickle, he purchased Carrie Carlyle's company. He laid off all the staff. And who does all the staff in Carrie Carlyle's company include? Carrie Carlyle!'

Charles was puffing like a dragon. He'd delivered the denouement in a single breath.

'So, wait, then what happened?' I said.

'Well, what do you think happened? I told Abbey the story!' said Charles.

'And?' the bartender probed.

Charles looked away like he was about to have a needle stuck into him.

'The most terrible thing,' he peeped. He looked like he'd just eaten earwax.

'I told her the story … and she had no fucking idea what I was talking about. She said, "Charles, I have *no fucking idea* what you're talking about."'

'And then,' Charles went on, 'I was overcome by a nasty little impulse. I'd spent about five whole days coming up with that story. I was irritated that I'd wasted so much time. So I just straight out said to her that I thought she could offer her opinion more often and that I found it suboptimal that she would ask my opinion but then have nothing to say on the matter herself.'

Charles' voice quavered as he spoke. A bead of sweat fell from his forehead.

'A-And then she said … that she completely understood what I meant. She said that she was sometimes too shy to offer her opinion because she was "in awe" of the way I so clearly articulated my thoughts. She had also grown up with an authoritarian parent who was not often wanting to hear the thoughts of his beautiful and spectacular daughter. At this I went crazy. I lost it. Not at her but at myself. I realised how ridiculous this whole situation was; that I couldn't even talk to my sweet little peanut and share with her my honest thoughts and feelings. That ultimately, this was all my fault, and it was all my fault because I am a coward.'

A tear dripped into Charles' Guinness. We watched him wail and contort.

'I hope you didn't tell her that story today, on Valentine's Day, did you?' the bartender asked.

Charles nodded.

The bartender winced.

'Yes … this was today,' Charles said, looking like he'd just sucked a lemon. 'I told her I was far too crazy to be with her anymore; I'd gone to cloud cuckoo land at some point after my birth and hadn't come back. I couldn't bear to be a burden on her anymore. I fled from her apartment. I dragged myself around for a few hours. Then it started to get cold and wet, what with the weather. So I came in here.'

Charles gazed mournfully down at the ground. We sat in silence for several minutes. The bartender poured me another drink and then moved away to clean some glasses.

'So, I must ask,' Charles finally said, 'what do you think of all this?' His physiognomy was riddled with self-pity and despair.

I went to answer but then abruptly stopped. Charles' story seemed to dance around my thoughts for a moment. I stared down at my knees as I really tried to think. Then I gave Charles my response, elaborated in a manner that I hoped he'd appreciate.

'I think you have a tendency to talk a lot and maybe that comes across as a bit too dominating. Maybe your girlfriend is also a bit more timid in nature. Perhaps you should give her some extra space in the conversation. Ask her a few more questions and listen a little more, you know?'

Charles gave me a blank look.

Then he erupted with a great grin.

'Ha, ha! Yes, perhaps you're right!' he exclaimed. 'Well I appreciate your honesty, William. But next time turn it into a story, my boy, otherwise I won't listen, I won't listen! ... Heh, I'm just kidding. I'll take what you say on board.'

'And one more thing,' I said.

Charles waited. 'Yes, yes, what is it?'

'Go make amends with Abbey, you idiot. Go!'

'Yes, yes, right, of course! Stupid, stupid – this was all stupid. Abbey! Abbey my dear, I'm coming!'

Charles leapt from his seat and flew out the entrance as quickly as he'd come.

I sat there for a while and chatted with the bartender while I finished my drink. Then I got up and went home.

You might ask what made me think about that night today. Well, in fact, it was my wife who prompted me.

We were lying in bed, sun shining through the curtains. My wife turned to me and asked me to tell her a story. This is what I told her, start to finish.

When it was over, her mobile rang. It was her friend Carrie who worked with her at a film distribution company.

'Hey, Abbey,' I heard Carrie say over the phone. 'I've gotta watch this Owen Wilson film tonight for work. It just came out. Was wondering if you and your husband wanna go see it? It starts at nine.'

My wife glanced over at me, knowing I could hear Carrie's voice through the speaker. She gave me a probing look.

I vehemently shook my head.

'We'll be there,' she said.

CROSSROADS

Michelle Porter

Rose had never been good at making decisions. It was always a long process, filled with torment and ritual. She wrote pros and cons lists, meditated, asked for guidance from a higher power and the opinions of family and friends. After all this, when she'd finally made a choice, she still found it hard to carry through.

It even manifested in her job as a journalist on a Sydney daily paper. She went into each story with big dreams and enthusiasm, only to find the act of writing it proved more slippery in reality. No sooner had she laid down a sentence, she was hitting backspace and trying to replace it. It was a tedious cycle that often looped back to frustration, before she eventually settled on some sequence of words to complete a sentence. Still, she couldn't give up on words; the pull to master them had shaped her entire life.

Rose didn't see it coming though, her life splitting into two. She was at work, stuck on a sentence, although fully conscious of the fast-approaching deadline, when her mobile started buzzing. Noticing it was Ben, she took the call, which she rarely did while in the office. At the time, it hadn't seemed important; they only spoke for a few minutes, making plans to meet for dinner that night.

They hung up and Rose's thoughts returned to the words on her screen and the need to arrange them perfectly. After hours at the computer, Rose looked away and checked the time. Her eyes widened. She was due to meet Ben in ten minutes. She rushed into the restaurant twenty minutes later and spotted him straight away, sitting alone at a table.

'Sorry,' Rose said, sitting down. 'I got caught up.'

'Hey, everything okay? I was just about to call.'

'Yeah, I was just working on a story and time escaped me.'

'What's it about?'

'A local cafe won a big award. Beat lots of other places in the state.'

'Should something like that take long?'

'I don't know. There's just so much material and it's a tight word limit.'

'How many words?'

'About 500. But I always sneak in an extra 50 or 100 words and hope the editor doesn't notice.'

'Well, I wouldn't overthink it,' said Ben. 'But I guess I'm more into visuals than words. I haven't read a book in years.'

'Each to their own, but I could not imagine that at all. I can't keep up with the books I want to read.'

'Yes, I know. I've seen your shelves, you addict.'

'Ha-ha, yes I know I'm addicted. It's a good addiction, I think, like writing. That cafe is going to bring in a lot of tourism.'

'Well, we'd better check it out one weekend then. But it sounds like we'll need to book in advance.'

Throughout dinner, Ben steered the conversation. He talked about the approaching weekend and activities he thought they could do, which flowed into a sketch of plans for weekends to follow. When dessert hit the table, he went silent. Rose picked up her spoon, but stopped when she noticed a large, silver ring on the plate of her blueberry cheesecake, along with a note with the words, *Will you marry me?* scrawled across it. She picked up the diamond and Ben repeated the question. She said yes.

They stayed out late, drinking champagne until the restaurant closed, before moving on to a nightclub for more drinks and music. While he was twirling her on the dance floor, she felt what seemed like happiness. But the following morning when she woke beside him, worry and an impulse to remain quiet, had replaced it. She decided to put off calls to family and friends, and kept her ringed hand hidden from view at work.

Rose was relieved to leave the office early that afternoon to interview a writer-director about his new play. She arrived at the local theatre on time and walked up the stairs to wait by the locked doors. Ten minutes later, a lanky man wearing a black leather jacket and skinny-leg jeans started up the stairs. He wore black, thick-rimmed glasses, looking like a modern Buddy Holly, and had dark hair, short at the sides but long on top. It curled over his head from an off-centre part and onto his pale forehead. Watching him move toward her,

Rose was enthralled.

He reached the top of the ramp. 'Rose?'

'Yes, I'm Rose, from *The Advertiser*. You're Cameron?'

'Yeah, but call me Cam. I always think I'm in trouble when people call me Cameron. Probably something to do with my mother.'

Rose laughed. 'I know a few people who say that. Good ol' Mum.'

'Have you been waiting long? Sorry if I'm late.'

'No, I haven't been here long. Just a few minutes.'

'Good.' He looked at her directly and smiled. 'Well, shall we?' He motioned towards the locked theatre doors. 'Don't want to get you in trouble with Mum, or your boyfriend.'

'No, no chance of that.'

***

In the morning, there was a new email in Rose's inbox. It was from Cam. Her heart quickened as she read it. He was inviting her to the play's opening and wanted to talk to her about coming to work for him. Rose had been waiting for an opportunity like this, and now it was here she didn't feel ready. She also knew this door, opening unexpectedly, might not come again for a long time.

It was with precision and fantasy that Rose dressed for opening night. As she slipped on a red dress and black heels and carefully applied her make-up, she thought of the night ahead at Cam's side. She had imaginary conversations with him.

But arriving at the theatre, the only traces of him were the VIP ticket and free drinks he'd organised for her. He was still missing as the curtains parted and then as they closed. At the after party, she stood alone on the fringes, watching others cluster together in chit-chat. She thought, *Ten minutes and I'll go.*

'What did you think?' The words seemed to rush over her shoulder from behind.

Rose jumped and turned. Cam stood in front of her, his expression unreadable. He clutched a glass of champagne.

'It was great. It was funny, and the themes – I won't say thought-provoking – it's a cliché.'

'Glad to hear it. I despise clichés.'

'Yeah, I avoid them at all costs – which, I've just realised is a cliché.'

He laughed. 'Don't worry, I'll allow that one. So, have you given any thought to working for me?'

'Yes, I have and I'm definitely interested. But what would I be doing?'

'Co-writing some plays with me, maybe writing up media blurbs.'

'Sounds great. But is it full-time? And when would you need me to start? I'd have to give the paper notice.'

'It will probably be more part-time and you can start after you've given notice – no problem. But I need to mention that the role's actually in Melbourne. That's where I'm based.'

'Oh, Melbourne?' Her thoughts were of Ben. 'Um, I'm not sure. I'll have to get back to you.'

He gulped some champagne, wincing as the frothy liquid hit his throat. He dipped his head at her. 'Okay, totally understandable. I'll give you a week to decide.'

***

The next day, Rose couldn't stop thinking about the decision she had to make. It had been a blur on her vision all day. It distracted her from talking with colleagues, and from the words in the story she was trying to get down to a deadline. The logical thing would be to talk to Ben, but she was certain what the answer would be. Then she thought of the alternative and began to feel nauseous.

On the way home from work, she diverted to the supermarket to pick up groceries for dinner. On the way back to her car, she had to stop at an intersection while oncoming cars whooshed through. As she waited, she noticed a man on a bicycle riding at high speed towards the lights. He passed through the intersection, then let go of the handles and thrust both arms into the air. His grim face softened and his mouth opened, as if he were releasing a deeply held sigh. On the other side of the intersection, he dropped his arms and let them dangle at his sides. Rose watched him as he continued down the road, hands-free and rushing into the distance. Envy tugged at her. She wished she could trust like that.

***

The week unfolded slowly, with Rose moving mechanically through the hours. By mid-week, she wasn't sleeping. Fatigue and a thinly-disguised panic pushed her to confide in her mother, who thought that marrying Ben was the only choice. Her closest friend listened and empathised, then reminded Rose that only she could decide what was right. With a day to go, she couldn't get out of bed. When she eventually got up, she called her doctor's office and made an appointment.

In the doctor's waiting room, Rose tried reading some of the old magazines jumbled on the coffee table, but she was twitchy and unfocused. Eventually, a door opened and a middle-aged woman stepped out and called Rose's name.

Rose hurried toward her and the doctor stepped back to let her through, then closed the door, securing the privacy that Rose was looking forward to.

'Hi Rose, nice to see you again,' Dr Ellis said when they were both seated. 'What brings you here today?'

'I haven't been sleeping and I'm so tired I couldn't go to work today.'

'How long has this been going on?'

'A few days. I'm exhausted, but as soon as I get into bed, my mind won't switch off.'

'Is something worrying you?'

'Yeah, I have a big decision to make … and I don't know what to do.' Unable to hold back and scolding herself for the failure, Rose started to cry. Breathless, the story came out in bursts.

'I see. Yes, it seems you have difficult choice there. Have you ever heard of a poem called 'The Road Not Taken' by Robert Frost?'

'No, I haven't.'

'Well, I recommend reading it. It's about choosing between two paths and the conflict, and sadness even, about not being able to take both.'

'And what … you think it can help me make a decision?'

'I'm not saying that, but it might help you realise that even if you make the wrong choice, all is not lost.'

'Interesting. I've certainly never seen it that way. I've had this belief that once you make a decision, that's it – it's over. I guess I have really black and white thinking.'

'Maybe, or it's just a different perspective. I think we can always make new choices.'

'Wow, you got all this from a poem? I'll definitely have to read it.'

Dr Ellis laughed. 'It's not going to solve all your problems. But I'm glad you want to read it. I can even find a copy for you now.'

After Dr Ellis found the full poem online, printed a copy and gave it to Rose, they spoke no more about it. Their interactions progressed in a series of brief assessments, and then Dr Ellis typed up a medical certificate.

Rose thanked her profusely as she left her office but, even so, emerged feeling it had been a waste of time. She went home, defeated, thinking only of sleep. But half an hour later, she was still awake, gazing into her darkening room. She got up, took the poem from her bag and read:

> *Two roads diverged in a yellow wood,*
> *And sorry I could not travel both*
> *And be one traveller, long I stood*
> *And looked down one as far as I could*

Like Dr Ellis, Rose sensed the narrator's sadness, but a rush went through her as she read the last lines:

> *Two roads diverged in a wood, and I -*
> *I took the one less travelled by,*
> *And that has made all the difference.*

It made her feel that perhaps the road she was meant to take was the one not expected of her, not forged by the wishes of others. It could be a mistake, an irreversible choice, but it also gave her some hope that the other path might not be completely lost.

Rose reached for her phone, and sent Cam a message, telling him she would accept his offer. Then she took a deep breath and waited for Ben to arrive home.

PANSY'S UNDERGARMENTS

RIC HAMBLETON

There was a time in Australia when corsets were obligatory for women of society. It coincided with a political movement, a shuffle of the bustle, which became known as 'the Mensen era'. My mother fitted and tucked the famous and the infamous among the well-frocked of Melbourne of this period. And among Mother's clients was Pansy Mensen. My mother became an unsuspecting ear to the insights and intrigues of the Canberra of the day. The thoughts and passions of the reclusive Prime Minister were shared with few but certainly his wife Pansy, and through her to the woman who shared the intimacies of her body. Or so the members of the Party would believe. They listened to my mother, Dorothy Marshal. A woman! Even the men listened. She became a kind or oracle of the Party.

I had been told time and again since I was a little boy that my mother's room was out of bounds. I got a good smack once for fiddling with some lace samples, but I could see no harm now that I was seventeen and not a nosey toddler. Still, I felt like I was trespassing.

There were bolts of pale fleshy pink and cream cloth, soft cotton stuffing, balls of white string, scraps and half-made cloth flowers, traces of lace, glass jars of pins, clips and clasps, arranged along a bench with her scissors in size from tall to small. However, the attraction of Mother's room just then was a wide bay window with a commanding view of the front garden of our home in Mornington, from where there had erupted a sudden commotion.

I had heard it from my room at the rear of the upper floor and raced to Mother's window. Two sets of neighbours were fussing around down there on the driveway. Father was present, Mother was clutching her cat, Uncle Dick rocked on his heels, the dog yapped in circles, and a young man in a fresh haircut and dark suit was dancing around some massive machine, opening doors, opening the trunk, lifting the bonnet, pointing and gesturing this way and that.

Then I heard my name called – 'Alistair, where are you?' – and I ran from Mother's room to the stairs, taking them two at a time in my rush to join my parents.

In the early 1950s, the British firm of Armstrong Sidderley Motors Limited created a large and elegant automobile they named the Armstrong Sidderley Sapphire. It was constructed from Hidumilium 22 alloy, which is suggestive of the car's nature as a rare and exceptionally advanced piece of technology. On its nose was a sculptural portrait of my mother carved in steel and plated in nickel-chrome. Or so I believed at the time.

The first of these beautiful machines had rolled off the Coventry assembly line in 1953. Then in 1955 one of them rolled into our driveway, crackling up the gravel in the late afternoon of a glorious autumn day, and quickly surrounded by an audience.

My father, Reginald Marshall QC, stood silently, poised and grinning, with his hands clasped behind his back, peering inside the engine compartment. The energetic young man who I learned was the dealership sales manager from Melbourne stepped back from the car, spread his arms wide and took a bow as if he was Mr. Armstrong or Mr. Sidderley, and then he shook Father's hand and bowed his way to the street where a Ford was waiting to whisk him back to the office.

My mother was enthralled by this beast of Britain, recognising instantly its status without any knowledge of its pedigree, taking this for granted by the glow on her husband's face, the reverent antics of the obsequious salesman, and the pure sheen of the coachwork.

As I said, Mother was a corsetiere, and a very fine one at that, building an enviable reputation across the fine families of Melbourne, along with a thriving business. The Armstrong Sidderley was hers, father's reward for her hard work and business acumen that had made her the city's most called-upon corsetiere. It was her fortieth birthday gift. It was her car. But she would never drive it.

'Oh my goodness,' Mother cried, fingers to her lips, staring at the machine in the driveway. 'It's beautiful, Reg. I shall have to obtain a driving licence.' Her voice faltered, timidly. She flashed her eyes at Father.

Father shook his head, his jowls wobbling.

'No dear, this is a finely tuned machine. Oil needs to be topped, petrol needs to be filled, and tyres need to be pumped. A boisterous and smelly business. It is yours to ride within, but a man must drive. Your brother Richard can drive …' Father glanced at Uncle Dick who smiled sheepishly.

'That layabout Dick!' Father continued with good humour. 'We'll make him the blasted family chauffeur, what? Earn his bloody keep, he will! Then of course, my darling, I will drive you at weekends, my dear Dot, and when Alistair turns eighteen …' Father touched my head and tousled my hair.

'Our boy here will drive you to your appointments.' I caught my breath looking at this beautiful gleaming creature in our garden. My future, my vocation.

Most memories of my childhood appear in monochrome, probably because they were triggered by black and white photographs. But this image, to this day is in my mind in full glorious colour embalmed in Kodachrome.

The coachwork was of a deep maroon topped with charcoal grey on the hood and bonnet. The chrome trim reflected the autumn light of the garden as though it belonged among the plantings, gold from the filtered sun and crimson from the massive maple that draped across the drive.

And there, above the grille was the sculptured portrait of my mother.

At least, I thought so at the time and was impressed. I learned later this was the Armstrong Sidderley mascot – a Sphinx. Their marketing was based around the line 'Quiet as the Sphinx'.

I laughed when I learned this. Quiet may have been the car, but not my Mother.

Her brother Richard once said, 'Dot could talk the hinges off a shithouse door.' This was my Uncle Dick who lived in the back shed at Mornington and retained the mannerisms and speech of his family's Footscray roots, to Father's despair.

Mother talked, gossiped, and prattled endlessly, in her acquired, refined upper-Mornington accent – a variant of the Toorak speech pattern engendered by the private schools of that wealthy enclave. A clever linguist could probably isolate the speech patterns, the nuances, as somewhere between Kooyong and Orrong Roads, maybe a bit wider, certainly a circle surrounding the schools of Merton Hall and St Katherine's.

Mother had acquired this mode and lost most traces of her native Footscray twang since meeting Reginald and mixing in legal, political and racing circles.

And of course, a proper voice was vital to Mother's trade. She worked at a time when Melbourne women of status cherished the corsetiere's essential, private and blushingly sensual service. A corsetiere was something to be. Your hands were clean, your nails immaculate, you moved within an inner circle, and an upper circle. You pinched, you tucked, you smoothed and caressed until skin and garment became one and your client would beam and sigh in pleasure and you would glow in the satisfaction of accomplishment. Oh, how mother loved her work, and she loved her Armstrong Sidderley and the independence and freedom it represented.

I turned eighteen around the time television arrived in Australia. 'What's wrong with the wireless?' Father said at first. Then he became incensed at Mother's insistence that I drive her to Frankston in the evenings and park the Armstrong Sidderley outside Veal's Electrics so we could watch the array of TV sets in the window, above the heads of the locals who huddled in blankets on the footpath. Father soon bought a large Astor television set for our living room.

Looking back, it was around this time that the corset business began to decline. I can't say there was a cause and effect between television and undergarments but attitudes and shapes were changing, along with the times.

Nevertheless, I drove Mother into the nineteen sixties, from measurement to fitting, from fitting to re-fitting, from Portsea to Brighton and inland to Malvern and Toorak.

As we drove, Mother would talk to me, to herself, to the world or, simply, to the beige felt of the ceiling of our beautiful English car. She would talk of the fittings and the conversations that went with them. She loved to gossip and when the events she reported upon lacked drama she would simply invent. Many rumours started this way and through retelling became acknowledged fact. She was politically active at the local branch level in the sense that there was not a scandal within the Party that Mother didn't either promulgate or invent. She loved being at the centre of politics and her craft was her entrée.

Naturally, she would also comment on the women we passed in the streets during our travels. Pedestrians, women struggling at a crossing with young children. 'Good God, look at the arse on that, will you!' was a common appraisal of the 'look' of the day, the professional corsetiere lapsing into her Footscray lingo, with a shake of her head and some tutting.

We travelled along the coast to Brighton where the women of the Party chattered incessantly at meetings about who would replace who in the cabinet, who would emerge from the closet, and who was the father of Cynthia's baby. My mother had an opinion on all, of course. She was a friend and a confidante to the wives' of the powerful, a shoulder to lean on, a sympathetic ear. My mother was an insider to the social fabric of the Party.

Perhaps she knew the father of Cynthia's baby, perhaps not. But she was known as the corsetiere to the Prime Minister's wife, Pansy Mensen, so the women of the Party tended to hang on her words. The men would also tune in, going quiet over their beers when Mother said something such as, 'Pansy was saying the other day …'

It was as good a means as any of learning what was on the mind of this shrewd and reclusive Prime Minister. Mother became something of an oracle within the Party. Her opinion was sought and she was the rare woman to whom the men listened.

I would accompany her on many of these visits to bowling clubs, Party fund raisers at hotels and private homes. I heard similar stories told in different ways, sometimes quoting Pansy Mensen, sometimes a cabinet minister or senior Party official with whose wife Mother had a professional relationship. I began to suspect she invented many of the stories and then attributed them.

Her clientele drew us out to Portsea where Harry Bolt, who had succeeded Robert Mensen, had recently been pulled under the waves to his death while weighed down with unresolved affairs of state and of the heart, which Mother would elaborate upon in a low voice while she tacked pins along a seam.

'Pansy tells me that Harold was …' She would begin, and her voice would lower.

'Oh dear,' her client would exclaim. 'Is that what was happening?' The pins were applied, and Dorothy would nod.

'Goodness me, poor Harold. And, oh dear, poor Zara. Or do you think …?'

Mother enjoyed these shenanigans and her status in the Party was good for business. I would escort her to the fashion shows and salons in Melbourne where she would mingle discreetly, maintaining a presence. Melbourne society was so close that once you developed a clientele, you were the only choice. It was necessary just to be there, as a reminder, so that your simple presence would trigger a particular response, often visceral, a feeling around the bosom or the bottom or the small of the back, a twinge at the tip of the buttocks that would suggest in mildly pleasant sensations that a fitting was due.

'Must see you soon,' Dorothy, Kathleen or Barbara would say. 'How's your diary for next month?' The little diary with the embroidered cloth cover would emerge from Dorothy's bag along with the tortoise-shell Schaeffer fountain pen, and the date would be settled. It was an honour, a privilege, a glamorous experience.

But Mother's world had an underside. Apart from trading in a fading commodity market – there were no futures in corsets – there was her younger sister Margaret who lived in an 'unimproved' housing estate on the outer edge of Frankston.

Mother would mutter something such as, 'Alistair, we will visit Aunt Margaret briefly.' And I would take the car into an appropriate turn off the highway. For a cup of tea.

I wondered why Mother felt bound by duty to visit her sister when they obviously didn't get along. I had heard Mother confide to Uncle Dick that her sister had let her down because she was 'common'. Then, on the other hand, one Christmas at Mornington, I overheard Aunt Margaret hiss to her brother, 'She thinks she's Lady Fucking Muck,' referring to Mother. Oh dear!

I didn't immediately understand the secret of this fouled relationship and put it down to Secret Sisterhood. But it had its own kind of ceremony. We would arrive at the run-down red brick joint in a back street that always looked like a garage sale; junk of all kinds plonked everywhere. I would sometimes have to remove a stack of roofing iron or some rotting wringer or worn car tyres so that I could park the Armstrong Sidderley in Aunt Margaret's driveway.

Mother insisted that the car was parked in the driveway, away from the louts, and she would not leave the car. Her sister would deliver the cup of tea and Anzac biscuits through the rear door and place them on the fold-down tray. As far as I know, Mother had never entered the house.

Once when I asked her why she hadn't, she replied, 'Why would I?' This was our family ritual. We would visit Margaret, park in the driveway and Mother would have her cuppa and a strained conversation with her sister. Perhaps it was part of her persona. She enjoyed travelling in the rear seat of the car. Her hands would be gloved, her face smiling regally and she often appeared to be restraining herself from waving. Urchins in Aunt Margaret's street would chase the car for pennies, flung from the rear window into the dust. Mother was awful like that.

But then I asked Uncle Dick just before he died, 'What is the problem with Mother and your sister?'

'You are the problem,' he told me.

'Me?'

'You. She wants your mother to take you to a doctor.'

'I'm not sick.'

Uncle smiled. 'Neither am I. Margaret is on about some electro-brain shit. She saw you in Bella Street, you know? Frankston is a small town. People talk.'

Bella Street, near the railway station, around the burger joint, was a meeting strip and pick-up. I had seen Uncle Dick there talking to some younger guys. He had seen me. He knew and I knew. And apparently Aunt Margaret now knew.

'What about Mother?'

'Dot knows your secret and couldn't care less. She loves you.' And Uncle Dick held out a shaking hand for me to clasp.

Dick died, Father died, the corset business died. Many of Mother's clients died. Every woman today wore a mobile phone and none of them wore a corset. Mother sold the house in Mornington and moved to Our Lady's Nursing Home along with the last of her clients.

I was left with Uncle Dick's shed and the garage, which were on a separate title.

One Sunday I picked up Mother for her outing, parking the Armstrong Sidderley at the front door of Our Lady's and helping the nurse manoeuvre Mother into the rear seat. We drove down to Frankston and she was silent, no chatter. Tired, I guessed, and I removed a crate of empty beer bottles and a toilet cistern from the driveway of Auntie's house to park the car, tooting the horn. It seemed absurd but Aunt Margaret insisted. 'Don't bother coming in,' she said, knowing Mother would never enter the house anyway. 'Just toot the horn and I'll put on the kettle. If I'm not at home I won't come out.'

I turned around and unclipped the tray table as Aunt Margaret arrived with the tea tray, balancing it in one hand while she opened the car door with the other.

'I think she's asleep,' I said.

But Auntie Margaret flung the door open with a cry and there was a clatter as the tray, cup and saucer and plate of biscuits fell from her hands to the gravel. I turned in my seat. Auntie was feeling mother's throat and shaking her by the shoulders.

'She's not asleep,' she gasped. 'Alistair, she's …'

I think I yelled something like, 'Close the fucking door,' and I revved the car, the tyres spitting gravel up the street. Ten minutes to Frankston hospital where a doctor confirmed that Mother had gone.

The next week Auntie Margaret came around to help me clean out Mother's things which had been stored in a closet at the rear of the garage. We unpacked bolts of faded cloth and a box of unfinished corsets. Auntie Margaret helped them out of the box one by one, feeling the fabric and the craft, then she laid them across the bonnet of the Armstrong Sidderley. She was weeping silently as she straightened them and adjusted the garments into a tapestry of pinks and creams and pale blues across the grey paintwork. Then she clutched at my arm and held onto the only living reminder of her sister. She gripped my wrist and sobbed into my chest. I put my hand onto her head and felt her brittle thinning hair, and I wept silently with her.

Today, I drive the Armstrong Sidderley most Saturdays, polished, tyres freshly painted, and decked with white ribbons. It now has a GPS mounted on the steering column. The old girl is always the lead car in which the bride sits silently behind the sphinx. Bridesmaids, flower girls, best man, parents et al, follow in a fleet of white Jaguars.

And just yesterday I read that the entrepreneur, technologist, and automobile maker Elon Musk launched his electric sports car into space aboard one of his own rockets. Inside his red Tesla was a mannequin – who was not wearing a corset.

I smiled at my mind's image of an Armstrong Sidderley orbiting Earth with my mother in the rear seat. Corseted, of course. Time flies.

MYSTERIES

GRAHAM WILSON

I live in an old house – well, at least old for Australia. I think it was built back when those who came on the first fleet were not yet old. It should be on the national estate, but it's not grand or otherwise remarkable, and so it seems to have been forgotten about by time.

The house is in an obscure suburb, not one of the well-to-do early locations like Balmain, Glebe, Redfern or the Rocks. It's in a gap at the back of old railway lines running west of the city, close to Newtown. It looks as if the railway builders knocked down all the houses when they built this line, and somehow forgot about this one. Perhaps a railwayman lived here once to work the signals, but if he did nobody remembers his story now. I have looked in local libraries, historical records of railways and other places, wherever else I could think of, but nobody seems to have bothered to tell the story of this house.

I know it is old because it's built of sandstone blocks, convict hand-cut, with chisel marks still sharp, held together with sea-shell mortar. The roof is slate, except for a small front porch with timber shingles, which leak when it rains. It's a house of only two rooms – one is my bedroom, the other is used for everything else – except for an outbuilding for a toilet and cast iron bath, clearly built at a later time.

Thirty years I've lived here, having bought the place of dubious provenance at a low price. The real estate agent told me it was a long-ago deceased estate which had gathered little interest due to its poor location, decrepit condition, and wedged between two diverging railway lines both long unused, kept apart by two rusty high wire fences.

Not even druggies came by; only mice, weeds and windblown bags found it a useful stopping place.

I had just returned from five years working in outback mines with a pocketful of cash which the tax man had no business knowing about. The real estate man showed me a freehold title, unencumbered, for this wedge-shaped block, six metres wide at the front, with a back yard twelve metres deep. I did not want to share my house title with a bank and this was all I could afford, so I paid cash and the man gave me the title.

I have lived here since. The title only dates from 1933, the Depression era, though the house is clearly much older. A friend who's knowledgeable in old houses, told me its features suggested a date around 1820, but who is to know without some real historical facts?

The house was not flash when I bought it and thirty years of neglect have not improved it, but it was all I needed and it suited my purpose. At odd times I thought it deserved a facelift but I had no spare cash to do it, and both the house and I seemed content to let our lives drift along the way they'd always been.

Then an old great aunt of mine up and died. Suddenly a cheque for thirty-three thousand dollars drifted into my bank account. I decided that using the inheritance to do some work on the house was a good option. I knew it would not go far in paying builders, but I'm still handy, even if getting a bit long in the tooth. So I decided to buy some materials to do the work myself.

I wasn't planning on pulling off the roof or anything big and dramatic like that but, rather, stripping out the basic internals and putting in modern fittings. I thought I might also create a private back yard and garden. I liked the idea of growing flowers and it isn't as if my neighbours would care, as the nearest are on the other side of abandoned railway sheds that line the road into my house. It's a dead-end road that almost nobody ever comes along.

Who am I? I guess you've gathered that I am a bit antisocial. I'm comfortable in my own skin, mostly reading old books, though I have a few mates who I share a drink with from time to time. We meet at a pub, and leave our own private lives at the door. When I was sixteen I lived in a little town in the back of beyond, but my mother got sick and died, and my father was already gone. So I came to Sydney to seek fame and fortune, both proving elusive. Instead I met a girl, another teenager, out on her own like me. Her name was Cecily. We lived together in a squat in Woolloomooloo and had a baby, a tiny thing we called Emily.

To help us get ahead, I took a job over the mountains for a fortnight, and came back with a thousand dollars in my pocket. But there was no sign of my girlfriend or baby. Our squat was empty and a few of Cecily's things were thrown in the street in a pile. Another man and woman, unknown, were in our place. They knew nothing about her or our baby; the other few people I knew around there also knew nothing.

I searched for a month in all the places I could think of but there were no clues about their whereabouts.

Then all my money was gone and I had to leave and find more work. So I went west to the mines, where I made plenty of money. I had hoped to come back and look some more for Cecily and Emily. But there was really no point. Gone is gone.

There was another special woman who came to stay for a while, but one day she went away too and never came back. Now, some-times, I pay for one woman of the night or another to relieve that part of my needs. I visit them at their own places rather than invite them here. For the rest of the time it's just me, in my home, alone. I'm well used to it.

Anyway, now it's time to get to work. My furniture is minimal so I move it to the back yard and cover it with a canvas tarp to protect it from the weather. The floor is covered in flagstones, old square slabs of sandstone worn smooth over time. Between them is a mix of sand and dirt with odd remnants of mortar. They're cold and damp in winter. So I decide they must come up, to put a dry layer underneath. I photograph them in position and put a number on each stone so that I can recreate the sequence.

I begin in the living room corner which is furthest from the back door, carefully lifting each flagstone free and stacking them all outside. It is slow heavy work and it takes two days until all are lifted and removed. What lies below is interesting but unremarkable – the odd buried coin or scrap from the distant past amongst the rubble, but there is nothing to fire my imagination.

I move into the bedroom and continue the removal. At first it continues the same, but half way done I find a block of stone sitting below the block I have lifted. This block is different. It is properly square cut, about two feet each way. I scratch my head and push on. Now I find that this is a new pattern, the old flagstones sitting on top of another layer of stone and those in this layer are all cut regular and square to the same size. I don't know what this is, but I am intrigued. So I remove the rest of the flagstones, brush away the loose dirt and look closely. These stones cover one half of the bedroom floor. They are all unmarked. I try to lift one free but it is jammed tight, as if wedged or mortared in place. So I take a picture. It's a little mystery but perhaps someone will know what it means.

It's Sunday night and getting late. Tomorrow I'm working in the local lumber yard. So I go to the pub to drink a few of the knots out of my muscles, and tell my mates about my discovery.

One, an old house buff, says, 'You need to let the "Heritage" mob know. It could be an old grave or buried treasure. They'll fine you millions if you dig it up without permission.'

I'm not a lover of governments telling me what to do but I see he has a point. I don't want to lift up the stones and find a heap of buried bones. Treasure, of course, is another matter, but that's the stuff of fairy stories, which only happens to somebody else.

So the next day I ring up the 'Heritage' mob and tell them a bit about my discovery. The person on the phone is only half interested, as if to say, who is interested in a bloody pile of old rocks? Though she also says something about needing an archaeological investigation. I can see all my money running down the plughole as a rich dirt digger with a degree gets even richer.

'Well, I might as well get to work myself and dig it up, see what I find,' I tell her.

This gets her interest and she says, 'Wait a minute, I will put you through to a Heritage Officer.'

A friendly female voice comes on the line. 'Kate here, how can I help?' I give her the potted version and I can tell she's intrigued. 'How old did you say the house was?'

'The title deeds are from 1933 but a friend in the know says much older, maybe 1820, though despite my best endeavours to find out, it seems that nobody really knows.'

'I would really love to have a look,' she says. 'Is it possible to arrange a visit?'

I can feel this getting out of hand and would love to run a mile; she has no details which will let her find me if I just hang up. But there is a sibilance to her voice that will not let me go. It's a sound out of another time and place; it holds a distant familiarity.

So, despite my better judgement, I give her a time and place, two days ahead, at the nearest corner pub in Newtown. She asks for my address but I tell her, 'The streets don't make much sense and it is hard to find. It's easiest if I meet you at the pub and bring you to show you.' I think that way I can always back out if needs be.

In turn, I hear reticence in her voice. 'This is outside normal procedure,' she says.

But she agrees despite her reservations. I like her for that. I feel a magnet pulling me towards her. Perhaps she feels it too.

I don't know what to expect when I meet her, though the moment I see her from behind I know it's her. She's sitting at a bar stool in the pub and has her back to me. I see her dark hair and trim figure, a woman in her thirties. A mannerism, as she pushes her hair back behind one ear, is redolent with familiarity, as if I've known her from before.

So I propose we both have a drink while she tells me about her heritage role and I tell her about the house, before I take her and show her what I've found.

She acquiesces though I can tell she is impatient to see it, not talk. I drink a schooner of beer while she sips her lemon, lime and bitters. I begin by telling her about the house and its dubious title, then about my inheriting enough money to do a limited fix-up. I tell her how I recorded the flagstones in their pattern before I began to dig up the floor.

She nods. 'It's good you have done that. Having a record of the past is important.'

I ask her about the rules before I go further, but she fobs me off, saying, 'Let's have a look first.'

So, to pass the time until I finish my drink, I ask her about herself and what led her into this kind of work.

I expect some meaningless answer but she turns to me and says, 'I think it is about trying to find a past that I am missing. I don't know who my parents were. I was found as a tiny baby, abandoned, and nobody knew where I came from. I was adopted and my adoptive parents are wonderful. But a part of me wants to discover the past I never knew. The nearest I can get to this is to study old things from the early history of this city; old houses, old stories, things that happened before I was born. I know it's not my own past but it is a way of me being connected to what came before, to build for myself a story of a past that I can put myself inside. It helps me make sense of my own private mystery.'

I nod, unsure how to respond. So I finish my drink and suggest she follows me in her own car, to see what I've found. In five minutes we are there and I show her through. He eye for detail is amazing. She points out ten things as we walk through the door and into the house that tell a story of its history. She agrees this house is very old, and she can't understand why it's not listed on the national estate as it's clearly one of Sydney's oldest houses.

I take her into the bedroom and show her the mystery of the stones that I've uncovered. She kneels down over them and studies them minutely, looking for quarry marks or other ways to identify them, she says. She's mostly oblivious to my presence, with total concentration on her work.

As she bends forward to look more closely, a small silver pendant falls out of the front of her shirt, swinging free on its silver chain below her neck. She stands and turns towards me, eyes alight with something important to tell me that she's just discovered.

But my mind is unable to hear her words as she enthuses to me. All I can see is the small silver pendant hanging from her neck. It has the name Cecily engraved, in connected silver cursive letters, mounted on a silver base.

I reach out and turn it over. On the back, in faded inscription, is a heart symbol and the words, 'From Jim'.

I remember so clearly that day I bought it, a couple weeks after our daughter was born. I did not have money to buy my Cecily a wedding ring, and our wedding was only a thing of our own promises, not a thing in a church, but I bought this pendant with the twenty dollars I had saved, and I gave it to Cecily with all my love. She had shyly taken it from me and hung it round her neck, where it stayed when she went away for good. Now it's returned.

Kate is looking at me, puzzled. I have not spoken. Instead I take her hand and lead her over to the mantel piece where there is a small black and white photo, in a plain frame, of a young woman and a tiny baby. It is the only photo of Cecily I have and it remains my most treasured possession.

I pick up the photo and hand it to Kate, saying, 'This is Cecily. This is your mother.'

The information she has to tell me about the heritage of my house is lost in insignificance compared with the living history we've just discovered together.

BITTERFELD

Patricia Ruell

January 1945. Pless, Poland.

Under the overcast sky the ground was covered with snow. It was almost dusk when Christa sat down on a stone seat in the garden behind the building that housed both the department store that was the family business and their home. She liked to pause in the garden at the end of a busy day spent helping in her father's store, selling everything from light bulbs to dresses. The stillness and the cool evening air was a pleasant change from the hot stuffiness of their apartment that always carried traces of her mother's latest French perfume. The previous evening in the garden, she had glimpsed a fox, but tonight all seemed quiet.

Just then she caught sight of Maria coming out of a rear door of the house.

'Christa! Your mother has been looking everywhere for you!' The white Spitz dog with Maria, that was a favourite of Christa's, walked over for a pat.

'What's happening? I've only just finished working.'

'You have to help pack. The family is leaving early tomorrow.'

'Tomorrow! But that is much too soon.'

She paused, knowing that she should not speak freely in front of Maria who was a servant. The girl looked young for her sixteen years with long blonde hair in a single plait. She had been working with the family for six months.

Christa beckoned for the dog to follow, and pulled her woollen coat edged with fur more tightly around herself. 'I'll go and ask

Mama.'

She paused as they walked inside together and brushed the snow off their shoes.

'Is there any hot cocoa? I'd love a cup,' Christa asked, and Maria went off to make some.

Christa's mother was walking down the hallway on a maroon and gold rug. She was a short woman with dark brown hair and eyes.

'Oh, there you are …' she began. Christa could tell she had been crying. 'There's no time. We've just heard that the Russians will be here in a day. We must leave very early tomorrow. Your father has been arranging for some wagons to take us west. We must start packing straight away.'

'But to leave Pless! Where are we going? Will it be for long?'

'Too many questions. Have your hot drink and get Maria to help you pack some things.'

After drinking her mug of hot chocolate, Christa went up to her bedroom, that she loved, as it was decorated with silk curtains and floral wallpaper. She opened her jewellery box covered in rich red velvet and took out her diamond and sapphire ring that sparkled in the lamplight.

'It seems so long since I've heard from Frederick,' she said to Maria who was already in the room, busy folding some clothes and putting them in the suitcase in the middle of the room.

'You must miss him,' Maria said. 'Where is he fighting?'

'I had a letter from him a couple of months ago when he was based somewhere on the Western Front. He wrote that he hoped we could get married the next time he has leave.' She had known Frederick all her childhood as his family lived not far away in a large house with a beautiful garden. It had been the suggestion of both their families that they become engaged.

Christa quickly moved all her rings, along with her silver and gold chains and brooches, into a velvet bag which would be easy to conceal. The family stopped for a quick meal of soup and bread before continuing to supervise the packing. Their wagons were lined up outside in the town square, illuminated by the light of the moon. Several men, their breath condensing in the cold night air, were feeding the horses some hay. As the night wore on and the moon slipped past the horizon, the horses hitched to the carriages occasionally snorted and swished their tails.

Christa slept deeply, tired out from helping with the packing.

It was still dark when Maria came into her room and turned on the light. 'Time to get up,' the girl said, placing a cup of tea next to Christa's bed.

The family did not wait for breakfast, but decided to eat on the way. They were warmly dressed, standing on the street next to the eleven wagons which were now full of the family's possessions. There were five children, with Christa the oldest at twenty and Peter the youngest at six. Christa climbed into a wagon with Maria, and they made themselves comfortable with blankets, scarves and hats. It was very cold and draughty in the wagons as they moved down the street, Christa looking back at their apartment, confident that they would be returning soon – when the war had ended. This was their home after all. She had lived in Pless all her life.

The roads were potholed and the snow made the family's progress slow. There was a constant stream of traffic moving west: people on foot wheeling small barrows, other wagons, and the occasional car. Most days they only made about fifteen kilometres' progress. They slept in the wagons partly to protect them, and partly because there was nowhere else to stay. As they headed west into Germany, there were more Allied planes flying overhead, and by the third week a plane swept down and dropped a bomb on two of the wagons at the back of the convoy. Another wagon was stolen during the night; while another four wagons were driven off by the Polish men Papa had hired, and were not seen again. After six weeks, there were four wagons left and the horses were getting tired. One child had a worrying cough and a fever. They were nearing a town called Bitterfeld and decided they would stay there for a while. Two weeks later they were starting to settle into their new life in Bitterfeld.

'Maria, can you help me? Christa asked one afternoon. 'I want to learn how to make some dumplings with the last of the potatoes.'

As Maria found the grater and a pan large enough to make potato knodel, Christa looked around the room that was now their home. It was very crowded for eight people. The two brothers and two younger sisters shared a bed, while Christa had her own bed, and Maria slept on the sofa. It was still snowing outside, and they kept their small coal stove going night and day to keep the room warm, although Papa worried that their supply of coal was getting low. There was a laundry tub in the courtyard outside that they would fill with water they'd boiled on the stove, and one toilet that they shared with people living in another four rooms.

Now the girls were working away, discussing the best way to make the dumplings, and what they would serve with them.

'We still have a tin of sauerkraut, and we could add a few slices of salami to it,' Christa's sister, Hannah, suggested. 'We have gone through so much food since we've arrived here. And the shops don't have many supplies.'

As she shaped the dumplings and started the water boiling, Hannah asked Christa, 'Have you heard from Frederick yet? You said you were going to send him a letter.'

'It's only been a week,' Christa replied, adding a pinch of salt to the water. 'The mail isn't very reliable. I'm sure I'll hear from him soon.'

Later, their father returned from his job working at a local factory and the girls proudly placed the knodel on the table, together with the sauerkraut, some salami and the fresh bread that Mama had managed to buy.

'A good effort, girls,' he complimented them. 'Perhaps we can have the same tomorrow?'

'All the potatoes are finished, Papa,' Christa said. 'And there are none in the shops at the moment.'

When they were clearing the table, Maria said quietly, 'I'm leaving in the morning. Your father made the arrangements. I will be working as a maid for a family living in Dessau. I'm catching the train.'

'Oh, Maria, we will miss you so much,' Christa murmured. She didn't want Maria to leave. There'd been too many changes in her life already.

'It will make things easier for everyone,' Maria said diplomatically. It was too crowded in the one room for eight people, and they were now getting short of food.

After cleaning up the kitchen with help from Christa and Hannah, Maria picked up a book and sat down with the boys, Hans and Peter, on one of the beds, to read them a story in Polish. There was a small kerosene lamp on the stand next to the bed that cast a flickering light onto the pages of the book. When Maria had finished, Peter called for her to read another book, so Christa brought one over.

Maria looked at the cover and made a face. 'You know my German isn't very good.' Maria had been taught in Polish when she went to school.

'It will be good to practise,' Christa suggested gently, and the girl haltingly read the story about Hansel and Gretel to the boys.

The next morning Christa and her sister Ingrid accompanied Maria to the railway station. She was carrying one small suitcase that she'd brought with her when she'd started working for the family.

'Do you have the correct travel papers with you?' Christa asked.

'Yes, your father organised it all.'

It was still cold, and the snow on the ground was dirty and starting to melt. The air was thick with smoke from indoor fires and there was a chemical smell from the local factories. Several houses had been destroyed by bombs and some shops had broken front windows boarded up.

'It seems so unfair that we have to leave our home!' Christa complained to Maria as they walked along the dirty street.

Maria stopped walking for a moment and turned to her. 'You are so lucky, you know,' the younger girl said to her. 'You have your Business Studies diploma and your family who are so kind.' They resumed walking and Christa thought about what Maria had said. The younger girl had neither schooling nor family, and for a moment Christa felt ashamed at her outburst.

The station was filled with soldiers and just a few civilians. When the train came to a stop, the sisters gave Maria a hug and wished her well. The girl felt thin beneath her coat.

'I'll write to you when I'm settled,' Maria promised, then turned and boarded the train. The girls waited another ten minutes until the train began to move off, and waved Maria goodbye.

On the way back Ingrid, who was eleven, started grumbling about the loss of her guitar. 'I know the piano was too big to bring along. But then my guitar was in one of the wagons that was bombed. I really miss my music!'

'You still have a recorder,' was Christa's response.

'A recorder! That's not a musical instrument. We had such a beautiful piano in Pless.'

'We certainly did. Perhaps when we get settled we can arrange some piano lessons.'

It was difficult finding things for the children to do as the schools in the area were all closed, and now Maria was gone, Christa knew it would be even harder.

As time passed, Christa and Hannah found work in the office of the local factory, while their mother looked after the children and tried to find enough food to buy for them all to eat. When the war was finally over there was a sense of relief, but that dimmed when they realised they were still not allowed back home.

Six months after the end of the war, there was snow on the ground again. Food and money were still scarce.

One Saturday morning, Christa was clearing away the breakfast things, and after checking their food supplies she saw that all the cheese and salami were gone; they had not had butter or eggs for weeks. She looked over to where Hannah was playing a game with the younger children. Christa immediately went to her bed and felt between the mattress and the base, and took out the black velvet bag that had held all her jewellery. After admiring her engagement ring, she selected a heavy gold chain which she slipped into the pocket of her coat.

'I'm going for walk,' she called out to the others. Her father was sitting near the fire, packing tobacco in his pipe.

Outside the breeze was very cold so Christa wrapped the scarf more tightly around her neck. She walked away from the centre of town, being careful not to slip on the icy paths. There was a farm with a small holding and a couple of cows, several pigs and some hens, about two kilometres from where they were staying. Christa knocked on the farmhouse door, and after a few minutes a woman appeared on the doorstep, her voice hard to understand as she had a bad cold.

'I want to exchange some jewellery for food,' Christa said, straight to the point.

'Well, you'll have to show it to me. If it's not pure gold, I'm not interested.'

The woman, who was quite plump considering the conditions they were living under, took the chain inside and examined it carefully under a lamp.

'Yes, it looks genuine. I can give you some cheese for that. I made it myself.'

And so it went on, Christa trying to get as much food as she could for the beautiful gold chain which had been a present on her eighteenth birthday. But gold wasn't going to feed the family. At last she left the farm, carrying the cheese, some duck eggs, a loaf of bread and a container that she had brought with her filled with fresh milk. She had to be careful on the way back that she did not fall over on the slippery path and break the eggs, or get robbed by another hungry person. So she loosened her belt and hid the food under her coat.

She was relieved to arrive back home with all the food intact. The air felt very warm after the brisk winter chill outside. She was unpacking the food when her father came from the back courtyard into the room with another man.

It took her a few moments to realise who it was.

'Frederick!' she exclaimed, seeing all the changes in him, how thin he was, wearing clothes that were unkempt, looking tired.

Mama came bustling over, arranging for them all to sit at the table. 'I'll make you something to eat,' she offered to Frederick, packing the food away that Christa had just brought back.

'You did well today, Christa,' she said, looking at the cheese.

Christa sensed a reserve in her fiancé; it was almost like talking to a stranger, and she thought at first that it was because they had been apart for so long. They chatted for a while, and Mama took over a sandwich and mugs of tea, with a splash of brandy 'to warm you up,' she told Frederick.

'Where's your family?' Christa asked.

'I don't know where they ended up when they left Poland. I plan to head to Bavaria where I have a cousin. I can stay there for a while and help on the farm while I try to find out where my family has gone.'

Christa wondered what his plans were for them to be married.

'I could join you when things are more settled,' she offered.

He looked at her distantly. 'I can't get married now,' he said. 'I have nothing but the clothes on my back. The fine house and furniture, the gold, it's all gone.'

'I can wait until we go back to Poland.'

'I'm sorry, Christa. It's over. Our old life is over as well. We may never be able to return to Poland. I can't marry you now.'

Mama was crying silently where she stood at the back of the room, and Christa, seeing her, was determined that she would not cry. It was important to retain a vestige of her dignity, she believed.

'I'll get you your ring,' she said crisply, feeling icy inside.

'No, no, Christa, you keep it. You will need it,' he said, his eyes taking in the single room crammed with beds, the smoky walls, the washing that was drying in one corner. 'I'm sorry it has come to this.' He thanked Mama for the food, and left the room.

The day passed slowly for Christa, who remained in a daze as she helped with the usual chores and prepared the evening meal. Later she sat near the fire, her mind crowded with a kaleidoscope of images from the magnificence of their home in Pless with its gleaming oak furniture, to the flight west in the wagons, fearful of bombing or attack from soldiers or other desperate people, to the suffocating life they now lived in their single room, the outside air thick with chemical smells. Later still, when her mother noticed Christa was still sitting there, she climbed out of bed and went over to her.

'It's past eleven o'clock,' Mama said. 'You should go to bed now.'

Christa went to get up, then cried out,' My legs won't move! I can't walk!' She felt quite numb from the waist down. What was wrong with her?

Papa went over and carried her to bed, saying she would be fine in the morning. But next day she was not able to move from her bed. After a few days when it was clear that the problem was not going to get better quickly, the local doctor paid a visit but could find nothing wrong with her after testing the reflexes in her legs and her sensitivity to heat and cold.

One day Papa came home with a wheelchair. 'This will make it easier for you to get around,' he said, showing Christa the chair, which was well-made, with a leather cover on the seat.

'My goodness, where did you get this? It must have cost a fortune!' Mama said.

Papa shrugged his shoulders. 'I was talking to a man down the street and he had found it in a bombed-out building a few weeks ago. He sold it to me for a small sum.'

Christa tried the chair out and found it gave her a measure of freedom and independence. She tried to forget about the probable fate of the previous owner.

They took her to see a specialist in Leipzig some weeks later, and again he could find nothing wrong. He suggested hot baths every day to stimulate the circulation, stretching exercises, and for Christa to try to stand for a while every day.

'Hot baths!' Mama exclaimed on the train on the way back. 'Where does he think we live!'

It was not practical to have a hot bath every day as they needed to boil the water on the stove but, even so, Christa did her exercises every day. Best of all she could now go out in her wheelchair and meet the children after school, and run errands for her mother. To make a little money, she cut up a large cream linen tablecloth into small squares, crocheted around the outside, then embroidered a red rose in the middle, and sold the cloths at the market that was held in the town square on Sundays.

Every night since leaving Poland she had dreamed of the house in Pless, of the garden full of roses, fragrant with perfume, and her own room with the small sofa under the window where she used to read. One day Papa had a letter from a neighbour in Pless, saying that their house had been ransacked, with all the furniture gone and the carpets ruined. There were now at least fifteen Polish families living in their building. To Christa it seemed that Pless was now in the past, not the future, and she did not dream of their home anymore.

One night there was a violent storm with very loud thunder and lightning. She woke up thinking the war had never ended, and that she must go to the air raid shelter. She found herself walking away from her bed. She cried out in the semi-darkness and Mama came over.

'I can walk!' Christa exclaimed. 'I'm better!'

***

Eleven years later, Christa walked down the street in Hanau, not far from Frankfurt, admiring the geraniums in the window boxes and enjoying the pleasant summer breeze ruffling her dark brown hair.

She held the hand of her four-year-old son, Bernd, who had blond hair like his father. They walked upstairs to their apartment.

After unlocking the door, Christa picked up the mail from the hall table and greeted her sister, Hannah, who was busy making a cake in the kitchen. The apartment had two rooms and its own bathroom, and Christa, her husband Albert, and Bernd slept in the bedroom, while Hannah and their brother Peter slept in the living room.

One of the letters was from Maria, and Christa noticed the improvement in her German since she'd been living in Pless. Christa tore open the other package, while Bernd went over to the kitchen to see what his Aunt Hannah was doing. There were papers from the Australian government giving approval to migrate to Australia.

'Hannah! It's been approved! Albert, Bernd and I are sailing to Australia in two weeks!'

'But that is so soon! And Australia? Do they speak German there?'

'No, we will have to learn English. But Albert has a cousin in Cooma, and he says there are a lot of Germans there.'

There was much packing to be done, the furniture was sold and the two weeks passed quickly.

Their ship was filled with around eight hundred people hoping for a better life in Australia.

As the ship moved off from its moorings in Bremerhaven, Christa wondered at all the changes in her life since she'd been aged just twenty. She lifted Bernd up so he could see the people on the wharf, and they both waved at the crowd gathered there to farewell the ship.

A new life awaited, in a country where Christa would learn to stride with confidence.

KEITH AND MONA

LAWRENCE GOODSTONE

Keith had not had a good day at work. In fact, it had been a near disaster.

As Chief Executive Officer he'd felt the full weight of the Board's displeasure at the company's loss of market value on the stock exchange. He knew it was not solely his fault but the buck stopped with him and he knew full well that if things didn't improve, his position would become increasingly tenuous.

Consequently, as he climbed out of the lift on the eighth floor of his apartment block in Sydney's Elizabeth Bay, a mostly salubrious, inner-city suburb, he anticipated dark domestic clouds ahead given the mood that had permeated breakfast that morning. Keith's young adult children had flown the coop and the buffer they'd provided between him and his wife, Mona, had gone. The last twelve months had been as bad as it could get and Keith expected more fireworks over dinner. He was tired and dispirited and wished it was already tomorrow.

As he dropped his keys into a glass bowl in the apartment's small vestibule, he took a deep breath and wondered what minor infraction of the rules he would be charged with today. He picked up the post, a bunch of the usual letterbox junk mail and a copy of the local free newspaper that sat neatly next to the bowl, and gingerly entered the kitchen. There was a strange quiet which slightly unnerved him. Dropping the contents of the mailbox on the marble island where he and Mona mostly ate, he moved from room to room wondering where his wife was.

On the one hand her apparent absence gave him a sense of relief but for her not to be home at this time seemed odd. It was then he noticed an envelope on the kitchen benchtop. His name was on the envelope, written in what he recognised was his wife's perfect but annoying copperplate script. Immediately, he sensed he knew the content of the envelope but he delayed opening it and moved towards the drinks tray.

Acknowledging to himself that he was alone in the apartment, he poured himself a particularly generous slug of his favourite Chivas Regal. When he did this in Mona's presence, there was usually either a disapproving look, or two just audible *tut tuts*. After downing half the drink in one gulp, he sat and stared at the envelope in his hands with a mixture of sadness and resignation.

Eventually, he opened the missive and at once realised that his intuition had been on the mark.

Keith

I'm sure you saw this coming so it won't come as a surprise to hear that I've decided to leave. I've gone to my sister's so if there's any urgent family matters, I can be contacted there. Otherwise, it might be best if we left each other alone for a while until we decide what direction we want to take. It's obvious to me that going our separate ways is long overdue. Our children are well on the way to being self-sufficient. I've thought about this long and hard and I see no point in spending however much time we have left in this life, picking at the scabs of each other's foibles. I'm aware that in recent times, I've become someone I don't want to be. I'm not sure how you'll feel about my decision but I suspect it will be a mixture of anger and relief. I will never regret the one thing which we seemed to get right – our two wonderful boys. I hope, in time, we can perhaps achieve an acceptable level of respect for each other. There's enough food in the fridge and freezer to keep you going for a week or two. No doubt we'll have to communicate in time about practicalities. We should both contact the boys in the next few days and tell them what's happening. I'm sorry things had to end like this but I think it was inevitable.

Mona

It wasn't so much the content of the note which rankled him. Rather it was so typical of Mona to express herself so perfectly and in that damnable copperplate. She was always so proper. The way the note was written reflected her years as an editor for an academic journal. It read like a professional memo rather than a *Dear John* message to a husband of nearly three decades.

She was right of course. She usually was. However, anticipation of the event had done little to prepare Keith for dealing with it when it actually happened. What he did do was to top up his drink and sit staring vacantly out of the window. He sat like this for a long time and it was only when he noticed the light outside fading that he recognised that he needed to pull himself together and work out what to do next.

He made his way to the galley kitchen and opened the fridge. It looked remarkably well stocked but he had no appetite. Ignoring the various offerings which Mona had left him, he opted for a packet of cheese slices and found a fresh ciabatta in the bread bin. He then wrestled with the Nespresso machine for five minutes before finally making a black coffee.

In spite of a calm which had settled over him, he suddenly felt lonely. Surely he couldn't be missing the low level sniping which he'd become accustomed to. It was simply the quiet which disturbed him.

He drank his coffee and picked at his ciabatta sandwich without much enthusiasm. He consoled himself with the thought that he could watch whatever television channel he wanted without the usual clash of preferences.

As his mind wandered, he distractedly began thumbing through the *Wentworth Courier*, the local paper he'd brought in with the mail. He turned the pages but nothing much was registering. As he reached the last few pages, his eyes fastened on column after column of adver-tisements for sexual services. There was nothing subtle about them. Pictures of scantily clad women with perfect bodies were accompa-nied with guarantees of discretion and offers of any number of options to satisfy mostly male fantasies. There were also cryptic, text-based advertisements introducing women who were everything from busty to athletic, brunette to blonde, young to old and every ethnicity which Australia could boast about. As Keith's concentration began to focus, it was the words 'house calls' that caught his attention.

The coffee had not subdued the slight intoxication which the large tumbler of whisky had stimulated. As he began reading the ad-vertisements, a feeling of rebellion welled up in him. In all the years he and Mona had put up with each other's argument inducing be-haviours, Keith had remained faithful. Certainly at times he had been sorely tempted to break his marriage vows but a strong moral com-pass had stopped him in his tracks.

He was suddenly aware that he had nobody to account to. Pay-ing for sex had never been on his radar and in spite of the ever-in-creasing fragility of their relationship, Mona had never denied Keith his marital rights. If their sex lacked any accompanying tenderness, they were both considerate and the act helped relieve tension, at least for a few days.

The more Keith stared at the page in front of him, the more his sudden urge to do something outrageous took hold. He stood and poured what remained of his cup of coffee into the sink, strode into the lounge area and treated himself to another whisky. Feeling emboldened, he returned to the kitchen and began studying the open page in the *Courier* more closely.

Eventually, the wording of one advertisement attracted him. It emphasised a reputation for offering services to professional men. While his common sense told him that this was an appeal to a niche market of male egos, he allowed himself to fall for it. He also liked the suggestion that the services involving house calls could be provided by well-educated, classy girls of all ages. As he gulped down the rest of his drink, he thought, *Bugger it, why not?*

What then transpired is not what Keith had expected. Not that he'd had any experience to draw upon, but the advertisement had led him to believe that he would be dealing with the slightly more sophisticated end of the sex industry. Feeling a little like a schoolboy ringing to arrange his first date, he dialled the number and his call was answered by a female, high-pitched Asian voice.

'*Ello dis* Fantasy Palace, what kind service you *wan*?'

Keith was at a loss how to answer. He was inclined to end the call but the alcohol had gifted him with a degree of Dutch courage.

'Eh, it says in the paper you can arrange house calls?'

'We do *dat*. Extra fifty dollar on top of two hundred dollar charge. What kind girl you like?'

He was tempted to say someone with a nice body and a PhD but thought that the voice at the other end might think it a prank call. Instead, he answered hesitatingly, 'Maybe someone in their mid-twenties who is clean and healthy.' He immediately realised how patronising this must have sounded but it didn't seem to bother the Fantasy Palace's spokesperson.

'You wan' front door, back door, hand job, blow job?'

Keith swigged another mouthful of whisky. 'Can't I decide after I've met the young lady?'

There was a long silence. 'Look *Mista*, we need know what girl send. Maybe you *wan* special service like golden shower. That cost seventy-five dollar extra.' Pause. 'You tell what you *wan*. *Dis* not supermarket. Need know now.'

Keith felt he was in too deep to give up. 'Just normal sex.'

'Okay. You give me address and what time you *wan*.'

This was the moment of truth. Once he'd given his address there would be no turning back.

Taking a deep breath he took the plunge. 'Three stroke forty-seven, Elizabeth Bay Place, in about an hour.'

'You pay cash or credit *car*'?'

This felt like ordering a takeaway meal.

'I'll pay cash.' He was almost inclined to add, 'Throw in a garlic bread,' but he doubted the other party would get the joke.

'Okay *Mista*, girl be there in one hour. You have shower. Girl stay only forty-five minute. After that you pay more.'

Just when he thought the transaction was over, out came the verbal fine print. 'No hurt stuff with girl. Any hurt business, man waiting downstair in car. He come fix you. Okay, have nice time. Fantasy Palace open twenty-four hour. You call any time.'

Before he had time to respond, the line went dead.

Immediately, Keith regretted what he'd done. What if Mona had changed her mind and was on her way home? What if one of his sons made a surprise visit? What if any of the neighbours on his floor saw a young woman entering his apartment and put two and two together? Then it struck him. *I can do what I like. I don't have to answer to anyone.*

With that thought in his head, he knocked back another small shot of whisky and took a long shower.

This was all new territory to Keith. After he dried himself, he stood wondering whether to get dressed or stay undressed. In the movies, he vaguely remembered that in such situations, the man was frequently attired in a stylish bathrobe. All Keith had was a slightly moth-eaten, terry-towelling, food-stained job which would not suit the moment. After splashing on far too much after-shave, he decided on boxer shorts and a T-Shirt. He looked in the mirror. Not that bad for a fifty-eight-year-old. He had a slight paunch but a moderately sensible diet overseen by Mona, and the use of the gym in the apartment building, had kept him in reasonable shape. He still had a good head of hair and he was actually quite proud of his greying temples.

As he contemplated all this in front of the bedroom mirror, he realised that his *delivery* would be there in ten minutes. What if, when it came to it, his equipment failed? Surely these girls had experience of a sort of bedroom version of roadside assist? He began to think and feel that all this had been a foolish mistake.

But before he could pour himself one last drink, the downstairs doorbell sounded on the security handset in the apartment's hallway. Slightly unsteady, he made his way to the internal phone.

Adopting a deeper, more masculine voice than the usual one he owned, he spoke into the handset.

'Yes, can I help you?'

A surprisingly cultured voice replied. 'Hi. I'm Veronica. I think you're expecting me.'

Keith pressed the downstairs door release button and stood in the apartment's vestibule. He began to feel slightly weak at the knees. He heard the lift door open and footsteps approaching. His doorbell chimed. He put his eye to the peephole. He wasn't sure why, because it was too late to cancel the order.

Just then, his mobile phone, which was sitting in the kitchen, began ringing. Flustered, he shouted through the door, 'Hang on, I'll be with you in a moment.'

Rushing into the kitchen, he grabbed his phone and without looking to see who it was, he asked impatiently, 'Yes, who's that?'

'It's Mona.'

What followed could only be described as a deathly silence. It was eventually broken by the doorbell ringing again.

Mona spoke first. 'I'm just ringing to see if you're alright. But I think I can hear the doorbell ringing. Why don't you see who it is?'

For the first time in ages, her voice had lost its sharp edge. Keith ran his fingers through his hair. He was very slowly losing his composure. He felt tears welling in his eyes but couldn't fathom why. 'Why are you are ringing me?'

The doorbell rang for the third time, only this time more persistently.

'Look. I'm not sure myself why I'm ringing you.'

Keith could hear a catch in Mona's voice but she continued. 'Maybe I was a little hasty. Maybe before we give up on each other completely, we might try getting help – something we've never tried. Keith, someone's knocking on your door. Why don't you go and open it, then we can talk a little.'

The whisky had now caught up with Keith. His head was swimming. He sank to his knees. In the fog swirling in his mind, he tried seek clarity. Was it to be the phone or the door?

MADE FOR FUN

THEO PERRY

'Man suffers only because he takes seriously what the Gods made for fun.'

Alan Watts

Canros was an isolated, rugged coastal town surrounded by numerous bodies of water, some stretching for miles.

Overhead, white snow-capped mountains spewed down giant waterfalls foaming into pools of emerald greens and blues. Streams flowed into lakes alive with a variety of species, before merging into the deep ocean.

Growing up in Canros, you knew that going to church was a big part of the community life, a civic responsibility, because it would become noticeable whenever you missed a church service; that was a sure way to make yourself a target for a special 'blessing' of condemnation. It was essential to be seen. I was a part of that community, and my family made it a point to show up at church at least one day a week. My mother made sure my brothers and I looked good in the public eye.

After church, I would stand and ponder the disapproving glare of St Paul: *Why so unhappy? Everyone loves you so much?*

Crafted with such skill, the stained-glass window came alive through the vibrant colours of St Paul's robes of aqua blue and gold embroidery laced with deep crimson reds. He was covered in the color of blood. His right hand held firm the leather-bound hilt of a long sword, his left hand cradling a partly unrolled scroll showing the words, 'The Word of God'. As light passed through the stained glass, St Paul never smiled. Sometimes I felt like throwing a rock right through his face.

My mother would call out, 'Talon, come on. I want you to say hi to Mrs. Orchard.' There was always an introduction to be made.

When I turned fourteen, the priest asked if I would like to be an altar boy. I agreed because it was a great chance to do something other than sitting for an entire hour listening to how we were all sinners and our only way to salvation was through Christ. The best part of the service was always standing at the altar, watching Father Brady serve the imitation of the 'body and blood of Christ'. Sipping the wine and seeing Father Brady in jeans under his robes was the best.

Looking down at the congregation, I would see all those sinners not understanding the word of Christ, coming to church week in and week out. It's no wonder St Paul looked mad. The last time I visited the church, I looked up to St Paul, mouthing the words, *'Maybe it's time to use the sword.'*

My primary school, called 'Holy Name of Jesus', was where I met my best friend, Charlie.

Every day, before the first afternoon class, we had to memorise a passage from the Bible, so Charlie and I would sit during lunch, attempting to learn the scripture. Using a little inspiration, we always managed to add a bit extra to the reading. Before lunch finished, we would sneak into class to write the daily passage onto the blackboard.

A daily passage might read: 'Surely you know that you are God's temple, where the Spirit of God dwells. Anyone who destroys God's temple will himself be destroyed by God because the temple of God is holy, and you are that temple.'

Our addition would be: 'God is in you, you are the temple, therefore you are God.'

Charlie and I would sit in class watching the nun's reaction, then look at each other, trying so hard not to burst into laughter.

***

Finally, St Paul answers my question about unhappiness.

It's fifteen years later, and I walk out of a doctor's office with a speck discovered on my brain. But the doctor doesn't yet know what it is, as more tests are needed.

But I'm not going to wait for more tests. My faith will heal me as I'm a 'believer'. My religion is absolute.

I spend a lot of time in prayer groups. The Holy Spirit chose me to be cleansed, I believe, and I'm guided to wander the desert for forty days. I can be healed. I book a ticket to the Judean desert.

It's now coming to the end of my second day there, a dusty, barren place, with the heat of the afternoon baking the rubber soles off my shoes. Small black spots invade my vision as the sun's intensity forces me to look down towards the horizon, which seems to melt.

Standing alone, I'm thinking about how there are good ideas and bad ideas. Contemplating my decision to wander the desert for forty days now seems like a bad idea.

Grains of sand and pebbles fill my shoes, bouncing one at a time more in than out, as I take each laboured step. One foot slowly dragging behind the other; no direction. The only thing I got right was to wear khaki pants, a white linen shirt and a headscarf.

Feeling sad, I begin to pray, my eyes tightly closed as I try to ward off the heat. In doubt, falling onto my knees, fingers laced together, I lift my spirit unto the Lord, hoping to renew my strength.

I speak softly. 'In time, I will get there, I am sure of it. God, my dear Lord, lead the way. I place my life in your hands. I trust you will lead me to my riches. Your hand will guide me. I am willing. I give you my life. I trust in you. I worship you. I am yours. Amen.'

Swallowing dust, attempting to wipe away the sweat from my red eyes, searching for tears that never will fall.

As I look into the distant rolling heatwaves, a new well of memories arises. I feel the coolness of an evening summer's breeze and for some reason, my mind offers me more comfort than my God.

I recall conversations, like waves crashing on the shore, which wash away my previous thoughts of prayer.

My close friend, Charlie, the last time we spoke. I can see him sitting aft deck in a white sofa chair, arms and legs crossed as if he was a humanoid pretzel. Enjoying his tomato juice, and his expression was one of complete disapproval of me. As I sat across from Charlie, I was ready for his barrage of questioning, his trombone voice humming through the air.

'Hey, you're crazy, you know that, don't you?'

The yacht's slow rocking back and forth along with the clanging of squeaky hinges chimed in with silver bangles jingling on Charlie's wrist, as he pointed at my chest to emphasise his point.

'That's way too much jewellery,' I said, tilting my head in disgust. 'And is that a shirt or a blouse you're wearing?'

In one swift motion through the glow of lights, I gripped Charlie's wrist, my fingers clamping down so the jingling bangles warped into slightly new shapes and were finally forced into silence. The clanging of the boat's hinges now gave a solo performance – *clang, clang, clang* – as the craft continued to rock.

Charlie's brow furrowed; his wrist slipped away from my firm grip.

The blue of his eyes seemed to turn grey as he glanced up to see my look of determination. Staring right through Charlie, I had no room for reason, my own eyes flecked with red from lack of sleep. I stared directly through his very being.

Then I directed my mangled finger straight at Charlie's face. Yelling, almost desperate. 'No, I am not crazy. God will protect me. My service is to the Lord!'

Charlie's body was now pulsating with laughter, his big mouth open, showing his teeth, and his head nodding with each forced exhalation. He levelled his gaze back at me, reaching out so softly that I gently lowered my hand.

Charlie flashed a smile and began again to speak with authority. 'Look, this God of yours isn't real. It's all made up, and you don't need to serve anyone. There is nothing to serve! Hey, look, if you really want to serve, please, I ask you, be kind and get me another drink?'

Hearing this, I was ready to do battle again yet sank into my sofa chair and reached inside my jacket pocket for a cigarette.

While deciding if I wanted to smoke, I held the cigarette between my fingers, rolling it back and forward in a calming technique to soothe my anger, as tobacco spilled out onto the deck and was blown away by the wind.

My voice became a low growl, deep and raspy. 'Listen!'

'Wandering the desert …' Charlie paused for effect, lifting his index finger and pointing as if conducting a symphony. 'For forty days. It's a test of faith,' he said, placing a heavy emphasis on the words 'test' and 'faith'.

My head was nodding upward with each sentence.

'But Jesus walked on water,' Charlie said.

'Jesus walked in the desert for forty days under God's protection,' I retorted.

Cutting in mid-sentence, Charlie pushed his empty glass aside and sat upright, looking directly into my face, his tone serious, all business. 'Ask yourself, Talon ... I beg you. Let me get this straight, you're going to wander in the desert. But even if it is for one day, who is going to cure you?'

He sensed my rising tension.

'Your hope for a miracle is just plain stupid. Let alone wandering for forty days in the desert.'

Then Charlie stood, his voice sharp. 'It's not going to cure you! It will kill you!' The sound of the 'k' seemed to linger in the air.

Now Charlie's body visibly relaxed as he took a different approach, pleading with me not to be stupid. 'No matter how much faith you have. No matter all the things in any book, no amount of Bible studies. You've convinced yourself beyond any rational thinking.'

He moved around the table in an effort to get closer to me, exuding compassion and tenderness. 'You're not thinking straight. Furthermore, Jesus did not go into the desert for healing. He went into the desert to confront temptation. You know, the red dude with horns.'

He used his fingers on top of his head to demonstrate. 'Face all misplaced, nose out of shape, cleft lip.' Charlie took his finger and pushed his top lip up to touch his nose. 'He has a tail, you know! God's Son went to battle with that dude. The devil.'

By this time I was speechless, staring at his antics.

'You know, it's a brotherly fight if you think about it. All made up.' He paused, and the corner of his mouth rose in sync with his right eyebrow as he gave me a cheeky wink. Then he yelled, 'Wait!'

It was quite a performance – and all for my sake.

'Here's an idea. What if the dude with the horns is Jesus himself? What if he went into the desert to battle with himself?' Continuing with his pleading: 'And who the hell knows if that is even true?'

The memory of Charlie's concern, his fervor to dissuade me from this trip, all down to his love for me, seems more real to me now than this nightmare inferno of pain and torture in the desert that I've brought on myself. A gust of wind sprays sand into my face, bringing me back to the present moment and my obsession with moving forward.

My dried fingers move over my sunburned face, and the blisters swell on my bottom lip, growing like ant mounds.

The wind passes. So too my memory of Charlie.

As my shadow grows longer with the departing sun, I look around, never having felt so alone. My inner voice is telling me to go back, while another critical voice is saying I have to finish this trial, that it's the only way to be cured.

There are plenty of miracles! is my reassuring thought.

My old Timex watch shows it's 6 pm and I pull out my phone to confirm that time. The sun won't set for another hour and a half.

It's time to set up camp so I unravel my pack. I pull out my tent and erect it as it flaps in the wind, offering the refuge of shade. I can't help but chastise myself for being weak, murmuring, 'I bet Christ never had a tent.'

Thirty-eight more days to go.

***

The next morning I wake up, my body aching.

I see my skin has been baked as if in an oven. My lips, covered in blisters, have swollen overnight to twice their normal size. Each time I open my mouth the skin stretches and cracks, drops of blood mixing with saliva.

I want to cry but have no tears, my eyes are so dry. This heat will kill me. And so my questions begin: *How did I get here, and what were the signs? Who am I trying to fool? What have I done? Will I ever get back to civilisation?*

Now that doubt has begun to set in deeper, I feel crippled. The realisation comes that all my life I've been taught to accept without question the stories of Christ, to follow the teaching blindly, to believe only in what I so badly *want* to be true.

Despair envelops me. I know deep inside myself, beyond the teachings I've been imbibing for years, that I now have to make a choice, and make it this instant: go back to civilisation or die in the desert.

With this almost ecstatic realisation – that it's either civilisation or death – comes a miracle of renewed energy through the power of my rational mind. I scrape together my camping gear and give thanks to my friend Charlie, not 'God'.

Setting out, my fear turns to anger and anger to action. I'm going home.

My only thought: *I need to find water – now.*

QUEEN STREET

Kay Dunne

Autumn is my favourite time. Finally summer surrenders, the temperature drops and the sky turns from a cataract haze to an astonishing blue. Once the syrup of Sydney's humidity disappears, even exertion becomes a sublime experience, and so, I happily resume my morning walks, the long way round to my studio, down Queen Street.

It is especially beautiful in autumn. Lined with plane trees and maples, their gold and vermilion canopies are like my personal honour arch. The shops too, have always drawn me there, with their art deco facades, coloured glass windows, brass door knobs, and plaques, announcing auction houses, antique establishments and art galleries. Colette Dinnigan, Moss and Spy and other fashion luminaries also inhabit this avenue, setting trends in fashion fantasies, and once, long ago, Queen Street was where I met Carmila.

She was emerging from de Vere's Interiors. It was a classic encounter: Carmila, the woman jostling parcels; me, the man in a rush; a collision; parcels dropped; laughing eyes meeting across the shared retrieval of said parcels.

Carmila, who claimed her parents were poor. 'We were, Brian,' she'd protest, 'My father was only a suburban solicitor.'

'And your mother a doctor.'

'A lot of her patients couldn't pay.'

'In Double Bay?'

'We could only afford to eat chicken,' she insisted.

'We didn't eat at all.'

I would trump her every time. We'd laugh, a moment of shared intimacy, of souls in tune it seemed, but Carmila had no idea.

She'd inherited a harbour-view property. Mid-nineteenth century and a convoluted mix of colonial elegance and early Victorian excesses. Ruby, gold and emerald stained glass windows, towers, dormers and crenellations, flanked by a colonial veranda on three sides. It featured six bedrooms, a swimming pool, a tennis court, a parterre garden, and a Thai pavilion, added by Carmila in the first flush of her inheritance.

'There's only two and a half bathrooms,' Carmila would complain, sipping breakfast champagne from a crystal glass. But five years on from the Thai pavilion, Carmila was low on funds.

The week before I made my escape, she'd been at me about moving into her house. I was irritated with fending her off – I'd never promised permanence – and then she started in again on the bathrooms. She wanted me to help solve her bathroom problem. I had no great objection, but the timing was all wrong. This insistence on our living together. I needed time to think – there were other things on my mind.

I had tried to lighten the mood and had taken out my calculator. 'Six bedrooms and 2.5 bathrooms, assuming one person per bedroom, makes the number of bathrooms per person 0.41666 …666 …' I waited for her to interrupt; to laugh at the silliness of six repeating and more importantly, at her own absurdity

'For God's sake Brian!' She leapt up, blonde waves swinging, her Sunday morning robe swishing around her gym-perfected bum. My God, but she was beautiful and, as ever, stupid about these things. I reached and grabbed a portion of her derriere.

A snort of derision. 'God, Brian, you're such a man!' A pause. 'And a peasant.' She swirled towards the door, the air flurrying behind in the wake of her robe.

I didn't think much about Carmila any more, or my old life. And I had hardly ever thought of her in the last two years, but Queen Street was the bazaar of the Carmilas of Sydney and she did come back to me at times when I was there.

But I was safe at 7.00 in the morning. Carmila would still be in bed. It was my time with the trees, the sky and shopfront dreaming. I felt free. I wasn't watching myself, expecting the sky to fall in, or someone to correct me, or for me to suddenly feel left out, or its opposite, smothered. So, I was completely unprepared for the encounter.

I saw her before she saw me. Reflexively, I put my head down. I couldn't abruptly reverse my direction. Could I cross over the street? Not enough time.

As though there was something of infinite interest across the road, I turned my head, trusting my sunnies and the edge of my cap to obscure me. I pulled my jacket close, continuing the pretence of preoccupation as we drew level. We, and the moment, passed.

I felt my shoulders release.

'Brian?' The voice was quiet. Questioning. Tentative.

I could keep walking.

'Oh my God. Brian!' Not a quiet voice. A voice close to strident. A voice I knew could escalate to banshee without warning.

My turn towards her was slow. I said hello. Banal. Bland. I was never quick enough with Carmila. She had a mind like a school of sardines, ever darting here and there, so fast you couldn't pick out a single fish. But she looked delectable with her hair flowing silver against her ivory skin, in a muted sienna coat, an Alistair maybe, and matching boots. I could see her body was as toned as ever and despite myself, I felt an ancient urge.

I tossed my head. Her blue-ice eyes followed my hair as it flicked across my cheek. My laugh was self-conscious as the words blundered out. 'You look well, dear.'

Her mouth twisted to one side. 'So do you. *Darling*.'

If I could blush I would have, but I never have blushed. Fortunate I suppose, because mentally I have blushed my entire life. 'Have to go. Can't stay. Late for work.'

Hands on those expensively clad hips, she stood firm. 'You are kidding.'

'Not now, Carmila. I really am late. Maybe I can ring you.' I wasn't late of course and I wasn't in the habit of being late. I was a compulsive punctual in point of fact, unlike Carmila, and she knew it. I also had no intention of ringing her and she knew that as well.

'Oh, no you don't.' She grabbed my arm. 'It's been a long time and obviously a lot has happened.' She jerked me towards her. 'A brush off? I don't think so.'

Someone walked by.

She let go of my arm but my compulsion continued. 'I'm in a hurry, I have a job due to-day … an illustration …'

'For goodness sake, Brian. Don't be ridiculous. Don't be a *girl*. Clearly, we have to talk.'

A shaft of desperation made me look around. But there was no rescue from Queen Street's passing Ferraris and BMWs. I scrambled around in my brain for an acceptable explanation for my flight to Western Australia. To no avail. I couldn't escape by any means except physically running away and even if I did she could probably run faster than me.

I wanted to take her elbow and steer her away. I would once

have done just that, but it was beyond me now. My God, I needed to sit down to do this, even if Carmila didn't.

A grey wave passing across her eyes took me by surprise. Her voice dropped. 'Why don't we sit here?' She indicated the bench at the side of the footpath. Not really comfortable, but there was no way this talk could happen in a cafe among the breakfast set. People of small pretences. Not serious pretenders like me.

'So, then, how was Broome? Enjoy it up there, did you? At home amongst all those sweaty mining blokes?' A momentary pause for breath. 'Are you on leave? Enjoying a break in the big smoke?'

At least I now knew she'd heard about Western Australia.

I glanced up at the sapphire sky. I reminded myself I had hurt her. 'No, not on leave. I came back to Sydney two years ago.'

She seemed to be in no hurry to ask any more questions. Maybe she was enjoying my discomfort.

'You've been hiding yourself well,' she said.

'What do you mean? Hiding?'

'No one mentioned seeing you.'

A couple, in trackies and with grey hair, jogged by dragging their shmoodle, or shmutzu, or whatever it was. My gaze found the pavement with its layer of rusted leaves.

'So, how long …?' Her voice trailed off. I tried to sneak a look at her expression but I couldn't read her as she gazed off into the distance.

'I suppose . . .' she began again. 'I . . . '

'I've seen Caroline and Jason a couple of times.'

She shot a hurried glance at me. 'They haven't mentioned you . . . or . . . anything. Are they well?'

'Seem to be – expecting another baby.'

'Really?'

'An accident, I gather – but they're happy.'

'Hmm, have to be, don't you? Not much choice.'

We both watched the passing of the bus as the sun began to shaft down the street like a solstice ray in an ancient tomb.

'I shouldn't have just disappeared like that.'

She was staring directly ahead, across the street at Moss and Spy's and I remembered the last time we were there together. I had suggested the dress she finally bought. It was flowing with a gossamer delicacy, with colours cunningly entwined so that you couldn't tell where one finished and another one started. The fabric skimmed her curves and its softness with those pale mysterious colours made her delicate skin seem almost translucent. She had remarked on my taste, on my artistic ability. I wondered if she would approve of what

I was doing now. Could illustrating for advertising be called artistic? A bit of a comedown from architecture, but not the pressure. Easier for me right now.

The silence continued. Her back was straight and her face blank. Her tension was growing and I was just mean enough to enjoy it. I waited, perfectly capable of keeping the silence between us forever, holding out until she had the guts to ask.

Lulled by my Clayton's bravado, I was not ready for what came next.

'I always thought there was another woman, you know.'

Another woman?

She turned to face me. 'I know you denied it, but you could have told me. You *should* have told me.' The veil had gone. Icy and sharp were back. 'You just disappeared. I thought it was me.'

Her shoulders slumped. This was worse than the banshee. What was happening? I expected her to scream at me, not this mute, defeated nothing.

I panicked – I took her hand. 'There wasn't another woman.' She pulled away and I distracted myself from the embarrassment of the wrong move by adjusting the angle of my cap.

'No.' I tried again, putting on a firm voice. 'There was never anyone else.'

Her eyes were wide and moist.

'I swear it – I don't know why you would even think that.'

Her lips twisted and her eyes weren't wide and wondering any more. 'You really don't get it? Do you?'

She sighed, then laughed; a bloodless sort of laugh with sharp edges. 'You . . . *You*, Brian. *You* were the other woman.'

My back straightened and my breath hissed through my teeth. I smoothed down my skirt; my pretty pink and green floral skirt from Colette's.

A solitary cockatoo screeched its way down the street.

'Well then,' she started, 'how long … you know …'

'Two years – two years since I started the treatment.'

I sensed she was relaxing. It was the denouement now. She was leaning forward with her elbows bent in her lap and her hands clasped, looking at me, slightly swivelled from the waist, her smile crawling upwards. She seemed pleased.

'Hmm – so have you done it?'

'The operation?' If ever two words were unnecessary, they were. I knew what she was talking about. 'Yes.'

'So, it's not a passing phase then.' She giggled at her little joke.

Betraying myself, I laughed. But, what else was there to do?

She wouldn't understand; she wouldn't want to understand. All that mental agonising, a lifetime of it; the attempts to be the man I was genetically supposed to be; agonising my way to a decision; even the relief and release of the decision took an effort; the surgery, not just the reassignment but also cosmetic surgery, feminisation; the two years training in being a woman, still training, a lifetime commitment to training. As if all that was done with chameleon ease. Like putting on a new autumn outfit from Queen Street.

'Ha!' She scuffed at the leaves. I heard them crackle as they fractured under her foot. 'So – what do you call yourself? Not Brian surely.'

'Brianna.'

'Very feminine.' She patted her hair. 'Hmm – maybe a bit obvious, though. It's not like, Diane or Jennifer, is it? Brianna is exotic. Draws attention to … the feminine … you know? Is that what you want to do?'

She patted my hand which was on my knee. 'I'm only concerned.'

Her eyes did an up and down appraisal. 'The frill's a bit much at the hem.'

'It's a Dinnigan,' I protested weakly.

The kind smile oozed up her face. 'And your make-up.' Her mouth pursed. 'You really shouldn't wear bright red lipstick, you know.' There was a pause. 'And the cap?' She shook her head. 'No-o-o, too much with the floral – even if the colour does match the jacket.'

Oh, God! I was overdoing it. I was garish. Too much makeup, too many curls, too frilly a skirt, too feminine a name. Sometimes I hear myself going all girly in the company of other women, even though I know I'm overdoing it. But I wasn't an XX chromosome woman, who knew by osmosis, perhaps even from birth how to dress, how to behave, how to sound. Thirty years of secret rehearsals had not prepared me. My taste, which I had so generously and unerringly shared with Carmila, did not apply when it came to myself. I couldn't judge, I couldn't see myself with an objective eye.

'So, this is what was going on when you were with me.'

I said nothing.

'So, tell me – do you still like women?'

The air had suddenly turned cold. I shrugged. She ploughed on. 'So, all along I was in a lesbian relationship.'

Her laughter cracked the air like a whip.

'It wasn't quite like that.'

'No? Then tell me, Brianna, were you fucking me as a man or

a woman, tell me? I didn't sign up for a lesbian relationship. Well … well, what was it? Hmm? Because you sure as hell felt like a man.'

The whoosh felt audible as my spirit was sucked right out of me.

'How many other women did you string along? No bloody wonder you weren't married at forty. People warned me. You never lasted in a relationship. You had to run away after three years with me. No bloody wonder.'

'Carmila …' I told myself I had made no promises, but still, I had hurt her, wasted two years of her life.

'Carm – you're right.' I wanted to run again, if truth be known, but I was tired of it. I'd had enough of deception, self-deception in particular. 'Carm. I felt towards you as a man. I fucked you as a man. I lusted like a man.' I paused, trying to find the words. 'I couldn't continue because I wanted you so much. And it was all wrong. I was sort of disgusted.'

'You're saying all that time I disgusted you? Or all the time it was just sex? Or both?'

God, this was why I hadn't seen her, hadn't tried to talk to her.

'No, no. I didn't say that. I meant I was disgusted with myself, being a man when I wasn't, living a lie, being a slave to my hormones.' I was exhausted but I tried to give her one more thing. 'Three years is the longest, the longest I've ever lasted in a relationship.'

This would have to do. She had a truth she could use if she wanted to. She didn't understand, but then neither did I, not fully. I couldn't explain it any further. I didn't want to and, thank God, she seemed to have run out of steam.

I sighed.

She sighed.

We both knew that signalled the end and we stood together. Now what? I didn't want her to say anything about us being friends, or how nice it was to meet again.

'Well, at least I know. You did leave me for another woman, after all.'

I let her be pleased with her own cleverness.

'You couldn't help it.' There was an ever-so-thoughtful pat on the arm. 'It's okay, Brianna. It's better I know, so I suppose I should thank you for that at least.' She raised herself on her toes and kissed me on the cheek in a display of tenderness and consideration. 'Good luck, dear.'

And that was it.

I watched for a while as she headed in the direction of Ocean Street. She kept her head down and her hands in her pockets, her orange Yakasumi bag hugged by her elbow to her Alistair-clad waist, and little eddies at her feet, as every now and then she swiped at the leaves with the tips of her Jimmy Choo boots.

A laugh and a sob came out together, as relief and shame competed for dominance. I had been too nice. I didn't leave her for another woman, myself or anyone else. I left her because I couldn't have done it if I'd stayed. It was hard enough to face the truth myself, let alone confide in Carmila with her expectations of a high-society lifestyle. It would have unleashed wails of betrayal and suffering – her suffering. Carmila had no idea, and I didn't know whether I was too cowardly or too kind to tell her.

It was done now and it had only taken five minutes. Such a brief encounter. After three years together that was the best I could do. Five minutes to explain a lifetime.

Her figure had almost disappeared now. So tiny in the distance and so scrunched up. I wondered why she had been walking up Queen Street at this hour. Could she have a job? I suppose I hadn't ever understood about the house and her anxiety about the cost of its upkeep; its inadequacy in these days of high plumbing and privacy expectations.

It was over now. There was still time for Queen Street; for the trees, the sky and shopfront dreaming.

But Queen Street had lost its gloss and was never quite the same again.

THROUGH THE SHADOWS

Matt Jackson

The screen door clattered shut behind me. I came onto the front deck of the farmhouse, placing both hands on the wooden rail and gazed across the fields of high, sunburnt crops. Sage, the old blue heeler I'd fostered, followed, paws clacking on the deck. In the distance a smoky trail rose into the sky. A cigarette jutted from the first two knuckles of my right hand. After a minute I raised it to my mouth.

Signs like this were one thing I was paid to watch for, caretaking. Especially in the summer heat, where the air between field and horizon shimmered like the fabric of dreams. Easy for fire to catch, on days like these. But I knew the direction the dust rose from and the track it followed.

So I waited. I finished my cigarette, rolled another. Sage sat beside me.

I'd become used to waiting.

Soon a low rumble emerged. Sage's ears pricked; she stood and trotted to the stairs leading down to the yard, her tail high and stiff. The noise grew over the sounds of wind and grass, clicks and song of insects, until it became a buzzing roar louder than all else. I knew the source by the vibrations.

The line of dust picked up speed as it rushed closer. At last the noise cohered into a physical form: a bike and its helmeted rider, loose dirt spewing from the back wheel, shirtsleeves whipping around his arms.

Without warning the motor cut. Sage barked once and ran down the steps. The rider rattled the rest of the way to the open yard, slowing, a slight skid the only flourish as he stopped. He kicked out his stand and shook off his riding gloves. Sparing a moment to reach out to the old girl jumping around beside him, he scratched behind her ears. Then he dipped his head to remove his helmet. Long thick locks spilled free, greasy with sweat. He swept his hair back and away from his face with one hand. With the other he shielded his forehead so those green eyes could pierce the shade where I stood.

I nodded. 'Paul.'

'Hey, Danny.' The boy hung his helmet from the bike's cross-bar. He stooped to give Sage a proper rub to her head and back, then turned to the house.

I took another drag from my dart and stubbed it out in an ash-tray I'd fetched. 'Wasn't expecting you for a couple of weeks yet. Your parents know this is where you're coming?'

Paul shrugged as he climbed the stairs. 'Yeah.'

'They decided I'm not a pedo yet?'

'Nah.' Paul grinned as we gripped hands. It'd taken him a few years to find the light he had in his eyes now. Then again, when we'd first met I'd told him he was adopted after his real mum got murdered and his dad abandoned him.

I snorted a laugh. 'Sounds about right.' I raised an arm towards the deck setting: two thick padded chairs and a table tucked into one corner. 'Sit down, eh? I'll grab something. Coke?'

Without waiting for an answer I went inside. I returned with two glasses, chock to the rim with ice cubes and black fizz. Paul rested in the far chair with Sage already curled at his feet. I handed one drink to the boy, who drained it instantly. I sighed, handed him mine, then took the first back in. When I came out again Paul had hunched in on himself. He faced the fields, eyes hid in a visor of shadow cast by his brow. He might never have smiled in his life.

I sunk into my place, breath easing from me, and put my glass on the small table between us. 'So how's things?'

'Yeah.' Paul didn't take his eyes from the distance. 'Alright.'

I nodded slowly. 'Wasn't expecting you 'til later,' I said again. 'We're monthly, so week after next, right?'

A long moment passed. 'Yeah.' The word got swallowed by the still hot air.

A frown tried to touch my forehead, but I settled deeper into my seat and smoothed my face. The Paul I'd first met those few years ago came to mind. But I'd learned from the space between. 'What's been happening? Making the most of the school break?'

Paul half shrugged. 'I guess, yeah.'

'What've you been up to?'

Another half shrug. 'Gone to the beach. Hanging with friends. Y'know.'

'Still playing cricket?'

'Yeah.'

'How's that?'

Instead of answering, Paul lifted his glass and took a long slow sip, then reached his free hand down to rub a thumb between Sage's ears. I'd half settled on my next question when at last he said, 'Alright.'

'That's good.' I said it gently, to let the coming silence wash over us. I sat back further. The boy's gaze remained unchanging.

One by one I relaxed my muscles, from the bar across my shoulders, to the lines binding my arms to the chair, to my toes clenching the deck through my boots. I slowed the air passing in and out of my nose and calmness pooled within me.

Maybe five minutes passed like that. Maybe twenty. Time didn't mean much to these sorts of conversations, where talking becomes a skill.

When I felt sure enough the silence wouldn't break on its own, I spoke. 'What brought you out here, matey?'

That finally triggered some movement. Paul's whole body wound tighter, drawing his gaze to his feet. He opened his mouth. For a few seconds he might've been shaping words. In the end he closed his jaw and shrugged.

'Been catching up with your mates?'

'Yeah. We're hanging tonight.'

I nodded. 'How about that girl? Cass?'

Paul's face twisted, the lines there suddenly redrawn into a mask of hurt. The contrast of shadows deepened as he tucked in his head, if only by a fraction.

I released a breath from the depths of my stomach. Teenage boys really only have three problems, I'd realised: blood, mates, and girls. Enough to fuck anybody up. At least it was only one of the three.

My question stretched out. 'It's alright, hey,' I said quietly. My turn to watch the horizon. 'What happened?'

The boy stayed locked. He reached a blind hand for his glass, took a sip, lowered it to his lap where he cupped it in both palms.

For a few deep breaths I wondered if Paul would speak at all. But the air shuddered in then out of the boy's lungs, and he looked up into the middle distance.

'We were at a party.' His voice sounded small and naked. 'A ton of kids from different schools. They happen all the time.

'I mean … everything seemed fine. Normal. We were drinking alcohol so it was fun, y'know? And we had different friends there.

Plenty of people to talk with.

'I had to piss so I went into the house. I was in the hallway when one of the doors opened.

'She came out of the room. With a guy. I stopped. I didn't know him. Maybe I did. I didn't know. But they came out, and she was holding his hand.

'I saw in past them. It was a bedroom.

'I looked at her, but she didn't look at me. They just went past. I watched them all the way down the hall, 'til they walked out into the yard. Then I went into the room. The bed was all messed up. And it smelled like her.

'The rest of the party seemed … normal. It was such a mind-fuck. Cass came over and tried acting the same and everything. I dunno. I couldn't think.

'I asked her after. She said the guy was a friend. They'd just been talking.

'It didn't make sense. So I kept asking. She got mad and told me he's just a friend. We had a fight.

'In the end she said she didn't really know the guy. She'd met him at the party. They'd started talking, and went to the side of the yard, and he asked her to give him head, and …' He bit his lip into silence. His head dipped back down. The falling curtain of hair hid his face. Sage had moved her head so it lay across his right foot. He reached down to her again and for a time seemed immersed in stroking her skull.

I reclined in my seat, as comfortable as if I was riding in a broken rollercoaster cart. My whole body felt bound with wire which could be electrified at any moment. With a long, deliberate inaudible breath, I released my grip on the chair arms. I waited.

We three sat there together, the dusty fields open wide in front of us as the ashes of Paul's love settled. Behind his hair I heard him take a deep breath. 'We broke up after that, a few days ago. But she messaged today. Saying she wants to be together. And now she won't stop calling …'

The unspoken question stretched between the boy and me. For precisely three breaths I let it hang. Then, 'What do you think?'

Paul straightened suddenly and spat on the deck; Sage jerked and spun. 'She fucking cheated!' He glared at the wet spray barely a metre from my feet. Then, like the wind changing, he blinked rapidly, jaw loose and trembling. 'But … I don't know. I love her. And she says she loves me too.'

Again, I counted my breaths. 'Is what she did with that other guy love for you?'

His face twitched, eyes flitting back and forth, tongue licking his lips every few seconds. But I didn't just see how my words pierced the boy. They could've been aimed at my own heart.

'I don't know,' he finally said, voice lame.

'That what you really think?'

Struggle broke out on his face once more. This time he lost. 'No.'

We lapsed into silence, the only noise between us the tiny rattling of melting ice cubes in Paul's glass. Sage lowered her head again.

His voice came small. 'Do … you think it could work?'

'No.' The word resounded with the weight of nearly twenty years.

The lines of Paul's shoulders dropped like he'd been hit. His hands spread, spidered, clenched. 'Why not?'

'Reckon you'll ever trust her again?'

A pause. 'I might.'

'Really? You don't think it'll eat you the way it is now?'

'… I love her.'

'I know,' I whispered. I braced my guts as the thought I knew I had to say came into my mouth. 'But you can never love someone into changing themself.'

And as over the horizon the first hints of orange tinged the sun, Paul's hope died. His head fell, and tears bled from his eyes. One drop fell to hit the deck. He turned his head to the side, away from me.

With a start, collar jingling and ears pinned back along her skull, Sage rose to her front feet. She spun round until she put her head in Paul's lap. It drew a huff from the boy. He ran gentle hands over her head and down her neck. A quiet drip of liquid warmth opened in my chest as I watched.

We sat like this for a while. Finally Paul turned forward again, arms hugging his chest. 'I don't know what to do.'

'What do you reckon?'

He remained hunched. 'I don't want it to end.'

I let time flow between us. Three breaths. Dry as dust, I extended my voice. 'I think you know.'

Paul swallowed, nodded once. At this angle the cast of evening light turned his face into a mapwork of rock. 'Have you ever cared about someone so much it hurts? Just to breathe?'

'Course. I've cared so much I've spent every moment like I was on fire.' I drew my gaze in to the tunnel to my secret heart, and the gates beyond. 'It's shit. But it ain't normal either. Something good

117

shouldn't make you feel this way. It's a sign something's wrong, and if you're in pain and not learning you'll keep on being in pain.'

Each word seemed to add weight to Paul's shoulders and neck, increasing the dark strain on him. His head held steady though. After a few long seconds he lifted his gaze slightly. 'When she come out of that room … she pretended like she didn't even know me …'

'Well, repay it. Now she wants you back, pretend you don't know her. We all make our choices. They're hers to live with.'

Paul stared down at the dog staring back up at him. 'You got a smoke?'

I took my deck from my back pocket and lit one for each of us, first his then mine. Paul didn't raise his head, kept his gaze down. We each drew our sticks down to the butt. Sage had resettled herself on the deck. When long enough had passed I stood and collected the two glasses and went into the house. A few minutes later I came back with our refills. I also carried a wrapped bundle of thin tan leather, pinned under one arm.

I set the drinks into the same wet rings they'd rested in earlier. The bundle I placed on the table between us. Then I sat.

The sun sank lower, waking the faint haze of dust over the fields to a glittering shimmer. I lit another cigarette, held it out for Paul. The boy took it, sucked in a drag. Straight away he coughed and spluttered. Sage glanced up at him, and I grinned as I put the lighter flame to mine. 'Guess it's good you're not really smoking. Just when you're around a bad influence.'

Paul smiled. The effort barely tinged his eyes.

I leaned back in my seat and blew out a deep breath of char and ash. 'Let me show you this.'

Paul looked over as I righted myself. His eyes cut raw into his face, but the green pierce of his intelligence was hard and clear. While I lifted the thin bundle from the table and began opening it, as if I had pulled open the bud of a flower, he took his glass, sipped, put it down.

Within its folds I revealed a set of small hooks and blades, each wrapped in a smaller cloth of its own; a square picture frame the size of a paperback and still with the $5 price sticker on it; and a slightly larger slide of wood, about half its outer border straight and smooth, the other half overrun with carvings crawling over its edges like a growth of vines.

I spread the first two on the table, laying each down with precision, then handed the last to Paul. The boy took it into his lap, turning it back and forth.

'What do you think?' I said. 'I've been working at it the last few weeks.'

He rubbed his thumbs across the frame, first the smooth, solid grain that had given me the idea when I first found the block in the farm's woodpile, then the ridges of flowers and vines I'd been shaping.

He spent another minute studying it. Then he looked up and flicked his chin at the other frame. 'This for that?'

'Yeah.' I looked at the photo there. Same as every other time, I couldn't stop my heart from pitching.

A young woman held a baby. Both of them were caught mid-laugh, the kid with a pure, wide-mouthed glee, the woman's smile dimpling in a way that might be mistaken for cheek instead of her deepest personality. She had a diamond-shaped face, and a dusting of freckles that spread from the peak of her nose out across her cheeks. Her eyes gave the appearance of bruised gauntness, yet despite this, captured even in the picture, the blue of her irises sparkled like buried treasure. Except for a few small differences, she could've been Paul's older sister.

I looked back to the frame I'd been working on. A frown creased the boy's forehead as he ran his fingertips over the pattern.

'This … it's pretty cool.'

'Yeah.' I took a drag. 'Your mum had a tattoo just like it, all down her left arm.'

Paul grunted. He reached over for the cheap frame, slid it open, took the photo out. This he placed against the background of my woodwork. He held it in place there, eyes searching the image the same way he had when we'd first met.

I coughed, cleared my throat. 'She got it after you were born. Her nan and pop – your great grandparents – had a big garden when she grew up. She'd play out there, and when she'd had enough her and her mum and her grandma would sit out under this awning with vines all over it.'

Paul nodded. He sighed and set the unfinished carving back on the table, reframed the photo. 'If she was here now… like, with all this with Cass… what would she say?'

'Let me at the bitch.'

He spun around, eyes wide, then burst out laughing. 'Really?'

'Something like that.' The grin slid from my face. 'She'd say the same I did, I reckon. Cass made her choice. You can do better than that.'

The boy nodded, swallowed. His eyelids shuttered as he blinked again. 'I know I never met Mum. But I think about her, a lot. What happened. I miss her.'

It made my own eyes itch. 'We all do, son.'

'Do you think I'll ever meet my real Dad?'

I was quiet for a long time. 'Someday, maybe.'

Paul stayed a while longer. We talked about his rugby team, a trip they were planning in pre-season, the surf there, and how I'd been planning to go to Bali to learn. How Paul had an old mal I could borrow. The local spots we could go together. Some usual schoolboy drama that wasn't messing with his marks so much anymore. We even roused Sage for a half-hearted game of fetch.

Finally, as a gust of wind rattled the house and sent a wave rippling through the sorghum, I checked my watch. 'Probably time you head off. It'll be dark by the time you're home.'

Paul grimaced, then fixed his jaw. 'Yeah.'

The two of us rose, a groan escaping me as I stretched and cracked. We went down to the yard, dog walking between us, me making little comments about the bumpy ride out. Paul took his helmet from the crossbar and pushed it down over his head.

'It was good seeing you.' I reached out and shook his hand.

'You too.' He bent down to give Sage one last pat. 'When you moving back to the city?'

'Dunno.' I shrugged and glanced around. 'It's not so bad out here. Everything I need, plus a bit of honest work. But we'll see what comes up.'

'I'll ask around. See if one of my mate's Dads needs help with something.'

I smiled. 'Sure. Still on for our usual? Once a month, right?'

'Yeah.'

'Good.'

Paul raised a hand to his visor then paused. 'And Danny.' A shadow of his earlier pain filtered out of his eyes. 'I mean ... thanks. I'm glad I can tell you anything.'

I nodded slow – once, twice. 'It's alright,' I managed. My voice croaked. 'Anytime.'

His smile came back. 'See you in a couple of weeks.' He snapped the shield on his helmet down then straddled his bike. I thought I must be looking at the boy the same way his mother used to.

Paul fiddled around near the base of the crossbar a moment, and the thing roared to life. He rolled forward, away. He raised an arm to wave, which I returned, before he rattled down the dirt road.

I stood there until he'd disappeared around the bend. Then I went up onto the deck and stood, hands on the rail, and watched the dust trail disappear the same way it had come.

Eventually Sage scratched the door to go inside. I let her in, then returned to my chair. The sun dipped lower on the horizon, turning the sky bloody orange. I bathed in the light for a while, sitting among the memories of friends and loved ones gone from view. And on the back of that, the few treasures I'd found.

Paul would be alright. Which is what was so sad. He'd hurt for a while, of course. But sooner or later they'd stop talking, then stop seeing each other at all. He'd find someone else to fall in love with and get his heart broken by. Same for her. Life would take them down different paths until they'd only think of each other in a moment, a curiosity of what happened. Time would steal their memories away. They'd never speak to or see or be around each other again.

And that would be it.

I looked to the photo of mother and child, so closely related yet coming into my life in such different ways. The symmetry of scars around my heart ached, as they always did. But as happened almost always now, warmth ran through them too.

Shadows lay long and thick on the ground. I stood, hunched over the table, rewrapped my work with the same care I'd shown opening it. Caught the ghost of my tired old eyes in the cheap glass. A few new lines ringed them, and their sharp green seemed no more than a blur in the low light. As I straightened I turned to face the open sky a final time, the regrets of a life swirling around my mind.

I tucked the bundle to my left breast. Then I went inside.

THE MIRACLE OF SIGHT

Carole Ingram

I wake to the blurred reflections of coloured objects.

This is unfamiliar to me so I blink to try to see more. My senses are soaring as objects become clearer. I see the blue sky through the hospital window, green trees growing in the hospital grounds, and multi-coloured flowers that decorate the garden.

Glancing down at my hands, I think how nice they look. My mother has been painting my nails ever since I became a teenager and now I see they are a nice shade of pink. 'Simone,' she would say, 'you have such pretty hands and your hair is so soft with a natural curl.'

I feel a tear run down my cheek, stinging my eyes, still delicate after the operation. The doctor must have removed the bandages from the operation while I was sleeping. I'm feeling overwhelmed so I get out of bed and walk to the window where birds with white wings are flying by. I'm transfixed by all the beauty before me and want to see even more, so I go to the other window which overlooks the ocean. It's so blue like the sky. I have flashbacks of images of nature from when I was about five years old and could still see. Soon after that, I developed shingles, which spread to my eyes and took my sight.

Afterwards my mother tried to keep my memory of sight alive by describing the colours of nature to me. She would tell me about rainbows. 'Nature is made up of all the colours of a rainbow,' she would say. Now, as I look at all this beauty I can identify with it again.

I gaze once again at the sea. Memories of how it felt years ago, so soft on my skin, fill my senses. Now I'll be able to go swimming alone.

My hospital room is quite small and sparsely furnished with a single bed and a tiny closet for clothes. The large picture window I am looking through is a blessing.

I feel a soft nudge against my leg and look down to see a tail wagging.

'Shane, hello boy. You've been asleep under my bed, haven't you?'

Bending to hug my beautiful golden retriever, who has been my best friend for the last ten years, I look into his eyes.

'You are so beautiful,' I tell him. 'I knew you would be all golden like the sun.'

He looks directly back into my eyes, trying to understand as he senses something has changed.

'You will always be my friend, boy. I can throw the ball for you to fetch now when we walk in the park'.

Shane puts his paws up on the window sill so he can see people passing by outside as well.

Next my curiosity leads me towards the full-length mirror in the bathroom. I was only five when I saw the last image of myself, with long, dark wavy hair worn in a ponytail. I was tall for my age with a slim frame. I remember my eyes were green and I had 'pearly' white teeth which people admired. So I used to smile at myself in the mirror a lot to see them.

Now, after what seems long years of missing my sight, I feel a little nervous and excited as I approach the mirror, wondering what I will look like. My first glance gives me a start. Here I am looking all grown up at fifteen. My figure has all the curves of a slim young woman. My complexion is still as I remember, and my eyes green. I smile at myself to see if my teeth are still white. They are. So, all in all, I'm happy enough at the image that looks back at me.

I make my way back to the window, which Shane is still looking through. I see a plane overhead and another flock of birds flies past my window. A startling green, red and blue parrot is perched on the branch of a tree close by.

'My goodness, Shane, it's all the colours of a rainbow.'

I can hear my mother's voice in conversation with a nurse in the hospital corridor outside my door.

I still have an image of how my mother used to look in my mind's eye. What will she look like now? I pray she'll be the same.

And then, there she is, just an older version of herself. An attractive woman with shoulder-length blonde hair. She's still slim, just as I am. She's dressed in a smart yellow outfit for this special occasion. She gives me one of the warm smiles I remember so well, and I run to hug her.

'I can see! I can see! I can see!'

The sight of my mother's tears is living proof of the miracle.

THE SECRET CHEST
OF JOSEPHINE'S GARDENER

Gabriela Dimitrova

1799, Mont-Saint-Michel, France

Dear Madame,

I am afraid that I am physically unable to come back home, as unforeseeable circumstances caught up with me at Rue Rambuteau. The frenzy of the market drove me into a quiet avenue, where I was falsely accused of robbery and maltreatment of a child. I am lying in a small prison cell in Mont-Saint-Michel, awaiting my sentence. The only thought I have at this moment is of you, the mistress of my dreams! I miss your delicate company terribly.
Your faithful slave forever,

Verne

After dropping the letter in the mail office, Verne went back to his cell. The inmate, who shared the cell with him, turned over on his bed when the door opened, and stared at Verne.

'What are you here for?'

'I don't know yet. I'm waiting for a trial for robbery,' replied Verne in a low tone.

'How long do you think you will be here for?'

'I'm not sure. But I am innocent, and I should be freed soon,' Verne said, looking down and back at the inmate whose body was riddled with both old scars and fresh wounds.

The tidal Mont-Saint-Michel, which held twelve hundred prisoners in 1799, was an object of awe and curbed pride for the French populace. The memories of the counter-revolutionists now were cluttered with sharp images of the grotesqueness of the place, made worse through the eerie echoes of the inmates' moans and the chill of floor stones caked with old blood.

***

Verne's strong physique was the outstanding feature that appealed to Madame Josephine Bonaparte when she first stood in front of his flower stall on Market Street. Yet seeing him then, she became acutely aware that she had encountered Verne somewhere before. Her servants were following her closely with their large baskets filled with fresh produce. *What marvellous, blue melancholic eyes*, she thought. Verne stood still in front of his stall, holding roses and honey.

'Monsieur, what a beautiful bouquet of roses! Did you grow them yourself?' Josephine asked.

'Yes, Madame. I have a little garden and a couple of beehives.' Verne blushed the colour of one of the roses as Josephine sniffed their perfume.

'Monsieur, would you happen to be looking for work? I can offer you a good place with a nice salary to work in my gardens at Malmaison Chateau. May I ask your name?'

'My name is Verne Charles. I would like to talk to my mother about this generous offer. May I give you an answer in two days?'

Soon Verne had accepted the proposal and moved to Malmaison from the family farm in Étretat. His mother decided to leave for Paris too, to work as a seamstress, as she was no longer able to sustain a living on the farm. Étretat was a rocky town but for Verne it was a place of the setting sun and marvels, so he had some regrets about leaving.

***

A knock at the low door of the garden shed at Malmaison surprised Verne. He hurried to answer the call, forgetting to put his brown wig on for the morning rose-tea ritual.

'Madame Bonaparte is waiting for her tea,' a young male servant called out before hurrying off again.

Verne headed to the drawing room, smoothing his long dark hair into a ponytail. His new life was now filled with roses, Armagnac brandy and Josephine. General Bonaparte rarely visited Malmaison, as he was caught up in the tangles of his endless warfare. Love letters from the General to Josephine came nearly every day, and Verne's jealousy grew stronger. He reluctantly read them out to her, and she could feel his envy as she regarded his flushed face. But she never took advantage of his deep emotion for a sexual encounter. He was her own son's age, twenty-six, and although that alone would not hold her back, he was a commoner, she would tell herself.

After tea, Josephine reached for a quill and ink to write a reply to Bonaparte as she sat beside an emerald lake in the midst of a grove of trees with leaves yellowing in the autumn sun. Her first two words on the parchment were followed by a long dash. Josephine sighed. The next line came out as a barrage of 'How could you think that I am unfaithful?' questions. What struck Verne, when at her request he read the letter back to her, was her ability to conceal her true feelings of resentment behind her polite pledge of devotion to Napoleon. When Verne finished reading, Josephine stood up and took off her large-brimmed hat, exhaling a cloud of warm, sweet air. 'Verne, I am going to have some rest,' she said, striding off to her quarters with her high-heel shoes clicking – a sign of her mood. She removed her trinkets and her diamond tiara and slid off her clinging satin gown from her shoulders, to climb into bed naked.

Josephine could not stop thinking about the resemblance of Verne to her lover, Hippolyte Charles, who had recently replaced her with a younger woman. Josephine sank into memories of her nights with Hippolyte, her nights of seduction, and slowly drifted off to sleep.

***

From afar, Mont-Saint-Michel prison looked ghostly and dark, but on closer observation, the layers of small and then taller buildings perched on the hillside signified the possibility of purpose and hope. Church bells praised divinity in regular intervals but could not wash away the desperation felt by the inmates. The choral chants of the monks added to the phantasmal atmosphere of the place.

Verne was awake before the guard's bellowing, which announced the start of the working day. Sitting on the stone-cold floor, motionless, his gaze was caught in the dazzling rays of the morning sun pouring in through the cell's barred window. Withstanding the misery of the place was only possible if he allowed his memory of Josephine to hold sway over him.

What have I done to deserve this? Verne wondered. *I have never offended anyone. God, have mercy on me! My only prayer is to see Josephine again before I die. Is that possible?*

'Hey, boy, don't be late or you won't escape the fate of your mate!' yelled the warden outside Verne's cell.

Verne shrank at the thought of the previous day's major event. He had been placed in a cell with a political prisoner of peasant background who introduced himself as Jacques, a royalist Chouan. He claimed his imprisonment was a set-up by a wealthy inmate who resided near the monks' quarters. Jacques claimed that, under his guidance, he'd escaped one evening to carry an important document to the local royalist group. But the guards caught him and brought him back, his legs chained and covered with still-bleeding wounds.

Verne had squinted at the bloody sight and cried, 'Jacques, are you okay? No! You are bleeding.' Verne started circling around furiously, not knowing what he was looking for. He blocked one of the inmate's gushing wounds with his sleeve, and with his free hand he poured water over Jacques to stir him out of unconsciousness. The wounds made Jacques wince in pain. He tried to pull himself up but slid down, cursing both devils and saints at the same time.

'Allez au diable, you dirty dog! I will find you, even if you are in hell!'

The next day, Madame Guillotine relished Jacques' bloody end on the notorious scaffold. He was declared an enemy of the revolution. Verne did not have to feign sickness and stay away from the execution, as he was already shrouded in a crippling melancholy, which had him sprawled on the mouldy floor, motionless. He gave in to silent prayers, eyes closed, body unresponsive to the biting cold.

***

'Madame …' Verne's face appeared as a reflection, a little speck on Josephine's psychic mirror. 'Sorry to interrupt, but your order has been sent. Your daughter is on her way here now.'

Soon the tinkles of the coach became loud, signalling the arrival of Hortense, Josephine's daughter.

'Oh, Verne, I was not expecting her so early. But I now have the pleasure of embracing my precious one even sooner.'

Josephine shone with love when she spotted her daughter. 'Ma chere fille! Hortense, how well you look! I'm so glad to see you again.'

She greeted her grandchildren with open arms as their mother, a plump and fair young woman, followed behind. 'My darlings, here you are! My darling Hortense, are you expecting again?' Josephine called out.

'No, Mama. I would write to you if I was. I have just been too busy to pay attention to my diet,' Hortense puffed, waving her azure fan too close to her face.

'Where is your husband?' Josephine asked, suspecting that he was with his brother, her own lover, Napoleon Bonaparte, in Egypt.

'Louis is not very well, but he insisted on joining forces with Father in Egypt.' Hortense lamented the situation. 'Father says that I should follow my husband to inspire him to victory'.

'Napoleon knows what makes men strong,' Josephine observed quietly yet confidently, smiling to herself.

Verne agreed with the empress. *She is right. My God, I'm a fool! Please, I beg, free me from the poison of my love for Josephine.*

As the morning haze began to lift, the golden light of the sun gradually formed a magnificent cloak over the green expanse of the chateau's grounds. It seemed an excellent day for a royal picnic. Verne moved swiftly in and out of the kitchen, filling the delicatessen trolley with cold meats and fresh strawberries and cream, along with hot chocolate. Platters of thinly sliced gold-skinned duck meat, with saffron gravy and hot sauces, and honey cakes with sprinkles of golden sugar would follow. Josephine always invited Verne to taste the food and drink at the start of her meal, before she began. Not that she dreaded poisoning, a danger Napoleon had warned her about, but she liked Verne's pleasing theatricality. Verne looked forward to this ritual, as he received his food to be tested in a silver spoon held by Josephine's soft hand. Today she decided to withhold this ritual, sparing her sunny glances towards Verne. Her concerns about Hortense must be his concerns, too, she decided. He noticed that Hortense was not only slow due to her being overweight, but her paleness was increasing as they proceeded with the picnic. Josephine requested Verne to supervise the children while she escorted Hortense, arm in arm, all the way to the sleeping quarters.

Suddenly, Josephine appeared back on the grassy field.

'Verne, can you call for the physician?' she called out. 'I think Hortense will need to stay on until she's improved.'

She sat to read a letter from Napoleon, which Hortense had forgotten to give her earlier. The daughter had impressed on her mother that she was being watched by the Bonaparte family. Hortense's husband, Louis Bonaparte, had heard some rumours that had made Napoleon angry over the previous week.

'My dear, Hortense,' Josephine had told her daughter. 'I have heard this before. But there's no question Napoleon's heart is divided between me and his duty to France, and he likes to keep it that way. Even his family can't interfere in his choice of me above all other women,' Josephine had replied, sounding so unrepentant about any infidelity she may have committed. Yet now as she sat alone, she was a little confused about the strength of her feelings for several men: for her soul mate, Verne, who she was becoming so dependent upon for his compassion and care; for her former lover, Hippolyte, who she thought looked so much like Verne; and for her husband, Napoleon, so passionate yet so often absent on the battlefield.

***

Verne's nights at the prison were very long – he prayed a lot, knees on the stony floor. He would wonder why there was so much violence in the world around him, *Are people deaf and blind to the beauty of music and nature? Why are God's gifts of love given to man going to waste? It can't be ... it is ... too cruel,* he thought. *I don't belong in this world. Lord, take me away from here!* Verne had sobbed at the sight of Jacques' crippled body.

He tried to recollect the events of the previous few weeks to find some rational explanation of his predicament. He remembered that after Hortense had left Malmaison, Josephine had walked to her desk and taken out her last letter from Napoleon. In the same envelope there was a tiny note, written in her handwriting, concluding with her own signature. The note was addressed to a Parisian artist in the most intimate tone and alluded to a face-to-face meeting. Josephine flung the note on the floor with a stern look and shouted, 'Verne, we are going into Paris to seek an audience with Joseph Bonaparte. There must be a way to stop my brother-in-law's vicious lies.'

***

Verne had Josephine's permission to wander around central Paris while she was occupied so that he could enquire after his mother's whereabouts. His memories of his mother were stirred by a child in the street pulling at him.

'Food! Do you have any for me?' A little boy aged no more than six stared at him with a gaping mouth.

'Oh, yes I do,' Verne replied, searching in his provisions bag. He broke off the end of a half-baguette he had stored there. 'What's your name?' he asked.

'Emile. I have a baby brother called Serge. He can't walk yet, but please come and see him too.' The boy was grateful for the crust and gnawed at its end.

Inside Emile's single-roomed home, the smell of mould, urine and gin hit Verne hard. In a large wooden box, next to the large iron bed, was a tiny sleeping baby swaddled in a blanket. Three milk-stained bottles were scattered near the baby.

Verne looked around and saw a chair, but no other furniture than the bed and the cot. Emile jumped on the bed and then sat on its edge, exposing his reddened knees through the holes of his oversized woollen pants, held tightly around his waist with black string. Verne encouraged the child to eat another piece of bread. It was getting dark when Verne heard a knock, and a hunch-backed beggar appeared in the doorway. Immediately the tramp was pushed to the side, and a young bearded man rushed up close to Verne to hold a knife to his throat. With his other hand, the intruder searched Verne's clothes, snatching his golden watch away and warning him to keep his hands together behind his neck. The intruder then forced Verne to swap clothes with him and led him to a nearby house, which he had just robbed.

'I will shoot you if you don't confess that you did the robbing, you hear me?' threatened the robber before disappearing out the door.

Verne headed for the door too, but was intercepted by two mounted police outside.

'We've got ourselves a novice bandit. Thanks to his slowness, we have the pleasure of meeting him face to face,' cackled the younger gendarme. 'Who are your accomplices? You wouldn't have been alone!'

They immediately hauled Verne off to the local court.

'I have not done anything wrong,' Verne complained, just as the real bandit arrived, along with Emile, to testify.

'Yes, sir, that's him,' Emile said, pointing to Verne. 'He broke into our house but there was nothing to steal.'

'Sir, I live at Malmaison Chateau and I am not …' Verne shouted, as the two gendarmes muted his mouth with a black cloth and tied his hands behind his back. They shunted him off to a cell.

***

When Josephine couldn't find Verne under the clock tower at the market, she shivered at the thought that something terrible could have happened to him. Soon Josephine's coach was on its way to Malmaison. She imagined that Verne was there, waiting for her, with supper steaming on the table.

But finding Verne's room empty, Josephine cried out, 'Oh, no, Verne! Did you decide to leave me?'

There, she couldn't see any signs of his intention to leave. *Maybe he's left a letter for me somewhere*, she thought. She opened a small wooden chest by the side of Verne's bed and with trembling hands lifted up the first of many envelopes she found. They were not sealed, and she unfolded the first letter to read.

My dearest Josephine,

I can't stop loving you and have the wildest of my dreams unrequited. Your grace and gentle nature have captivated the depths of my heart, and I am in a constant fight with the ...'

The next letter was from Verne's mother, received just before Josephine and Verne left for central Paris.

My dearest son,

I hope you can forgive me that I never told you about your twin brother, Hippolyte. You were only two years old when we gave you away to a wealthy gentleman. Our family could barely afford one half bread loaf a day in the famine year of 1778.

My love will always be with you. Your loving mother,
Marie Charles

Josephine's sobs could be heard as far as the garden. Next day she missed all her meals, drinking only hot chocolate. Her roses looked dull and sickly. So she wrote a letter to the Parisian police chief, enquiring about Verne, and waited anxiously for a response.

A week later, she received a letter, not from the police but from Verne himself. She sighed with relief. It was his first letter from the prison at Mont-Saint-Michel.

***

The spring of 1799 had only just arrived in Mont-Saint-Michel and the nights would come down quickly, to eke every last bit of warmth from the day. Josephine, in beggar clothes and with her face covered in soot, waited while her manservant, also dressed in ragged clothes, pulled a boat close to the river's edge near Mont-Saint-Michel, so that Josephine could step down into it. The moon's silver circle cast a faint light, muted by the dark grove of forest near the prison. Josephine's knowledge of the place had increased after she consulted old maps of the island town kept in Napoleon's library, as well as fictional accounts of prison adventures.

Despite her preparation, Josephine was afraid, as she'd heard about the 'enemies of the revolution' and the reckless policing of the population.

She was also worried about Napoleon's rising animosity toward her, which she felt was unjustified and presented a risk to her wellbeing. The question of divorce was hanging in the air, more threatening now, because she was enacting her plan for Verne's escape from one of the harshest political prisons in France. Her young servant rowed energetically, winding between eddies of water that looked like ghosts with many wrinkled arms. Toads took turns diving into the murky waters and the crisp air rose as a spiral around Josephine's body.

A dark figure on the opposite shore waved at them, in accordance with the escape plan. Verne was going to be free in an hour, with the exchange of some money for an 'official' pardon. The last letter he'd sent Josephine had described his great admiration for a monk known by the name of Rousseau, who secretly helped the poor inmates with food and medicine.

On the other shore, as Josephine stepped from the boat, she gazed at the monk standing in front of her.

'Madame, Verne told me all about you. He will be here as soon as the night guards change.' The monk spoke in a gentle whisper. 'God has him firmly under his wing. Do not fret.'

'Father, I wish to give you three hundred francs as a sign of my appreciation for what you have done.' Josephine handed over a black rattan bag to the monk, bowed and stepped back. The monk fell to his knees, clinging hard to the bag, speechless with gratitude.

'Father Benedict,' the monk called softly, as he turned towards a black prominent rock near him. 'I have good news for you.'

Just then, a hunch-backed monk appeared from behind the rock carrying a lantern in his hand. His martyred eyes seemed like two pale green diamonds, inspiring both awe and submission. He was mute, but his calm gestures indicated that Josephine should follow him. Soon they reached an underground stairway which led to the monks' cells. The air was moist and stagnant, forbidding any source of natural light. They were close to the meeting point with Verne. In the darkness, the younger monk climbed up a long ladder, which led to the south end of the prison where a church had once been located but was now a workshop for making hats. The first cell was Verne's. He was deep in prayer when the young monk appeared.

'Josephine? Where is she?' Verne gasped on seeing the monk. His sunken cheekbones blushed with fresh life as he jumped to his feet. A few steps and the two men were by her side.

'Madame … I have missed you so much … and Malmaison, of course.'

Verne kneeled at Josephine's feet. She cupped his face in her soft gentle hands.

'I am so sorry to put you through so much and bring you here to this dreadful place,' he said.

Her tears poured down her face, some even falling onto Verne's shoulder.

'I have seen a lot for the last few days, Madame. The poor people in here need me – here and now.'

'Oh, no, Verne, please, don't. I need you so much too!' Josephine stared down at him in dismay.

'There is only one way to happiness in this world …' Verne continued. He took in a deep breath. '… To give yourself in service for people's wellbeing. I have been selfish to desire you, knowing that I am sinning against the will of God.'

'Verne, I will never stop thinking of you, my soul mate! Malmaison would be such a sad orphan without you.' Josephine brushed away her burning tears.

'Madame, I have given away my manly desires. I have taken an oath of chastity and the vows of monasticism. I will always pray for you. Adieu!' Verne bowed, calm and peaceful now, before disappearing behind the dark door of a monastic cell.

From the tiny, barred window of his cell, Verne followed the sight of the boat carrying his beloved Josephine, as it glided down the river in the moonlight.

THE LAST
OF MY SANDCASTLE DAYS

DAVID BENN

A week before this last school holiday I was at my boys' school swimming carnival. Sitting in the top of the stand with the other parents, I was looking down at my elder boy, Harrison, hunched forward on a bench beside the pool with his back to me. Harrison had just turned twelve and was tall for his age. No longer a skinny little kid; muscles were emerging across his back and shoulders. He was sitting in his speedos, goggles pushed up on his forehead, as he called encouragement to his friends. The wispy Eurasian angel beside him, Holly, kept glancing across at him.

She sat upright, her black hair in a long, loose plait down her back. She stopped glancing and turned to stare at him. I could see two dark almond eyes fixed on Harrison's back. Her willowy brown body was budding beneath her bright blue swimsuit. I felt my interest becoming inappropriate and turned to see if her mother, Karen, was watching too. She wasn't. Karen was sitting a few parents away to my right, looking at her mobile phone.

I turned back to see Holly tentatively raise a hand behind my son's back and lightly place it on his shoulder. And there! She gave him one gentle curious squeeze. Harrison kept calling out to his friends. She dropped her hand and placed it in her lap. Harrison stood and walked down the pool to join the next race. He won three out of the four subsequent events.

He doesn't do swim squads; apparently he doesn't have to.

Harrison's brother James is only a year younger but he is still what I would call 'little'. He pushes his hair forward; his heavy fringe brushes the top of his large dark eyes. I sometimes wake at night to find him curled up beside me in bed. A thumb stuck in his mouth. He loves showing me his favourite toys when we go shopping. His eyes blink away tears if we run out of Coco Pops and he loves building sandcastles.

***

The small sunny corner of beach north of Greenmount is a haven for my children. Protected from cool southerly winds and swells, the sparkling water is clean and shallow. From out of the great blue Pacific Ocean, smooth, well-rounded waves roll into the beach and wash up onto the talcum sand.

James and I have spent day after day chasing each other around the basalt boulders of the headland, splashing in the shallows and rock pools, and building sandcastles. Sitting together on the beach, just past the reach of the waves, we build great walls and spires of wet sand with the bursting Queensland sun drying the salt water on our bodies. Our skin is warm and sticky. Our hair is dry and crisp.

This morning at Greenmount he is dressed in his bright green rash vest with his spindly little legs poking out of his matching bright green elastic-waisted board shorts. We are sitting at the very edge of the waves. Our hands tunnel beneath the sand until we meet. I grab his fingers, pulling his arm into the tunnel. He squeals and laughs, trying to wriggle free as frothy white water runs around us.

Harrison no longer builds sandcastles. He is body surfing out beyond the white water. He launches onto a curling crystal wave, which speeds him into the shallows. Running out of the swirling wash towards us, he is wearing his favourite board shorts; black and blue, pulled tight, low on his hips. No rash vest. With his hands on his hips, he stands over me panting. 'Dad! What are you sitting here for? Come for a swim!'

James looks at me and I ask, 'Will you be right here for a bit if I go for a swim with Harrison?' James looks down at the sand. 'Perhaps you'd like to come with us?' I suggest.

James hates it when I leave him by himself. He has only just stopped asking me to move back into the family home. He looks apprehensively at the waves crashing in the shallows and, after a few seconds, the greater fear wins his decision.

He looks back down at the sand. 'No, I'll stay here,' he says quietly.

'Okay, I won't be too long.' I don't like giving James an anxious little choice. It's his holiday. But it's Harrison's holiday, too. Both boys need my time. Both boys need my attention.

Harrison and I run into the surging, white water. He latches onto my arm and I pull him through the waves, only letting go so we can dive under the curling white slabs. Together we swim, plunging under the crashing waves out to where the water is deep and clear. We rise and fall on the smooth, rolling humps. I can just touch the sandy bottom in the valleys. At the crest, the water is three feet over my head.

Harrison loves a competition. 'Let's catch one together and have a race. Okay, Dad? I'll tell you which one'.

He treads water, trying to lift his head to see over the small, undulating curves. He lets them all pass before a larger wave, smooth and steep, rises before us and starts to crest. 'This one, Dad! This one!'

I swim as hard as I can onto its curling blue face. I quickly shoot a glance sideways. The wave has picked up Harrison and is throwing him towards the beach. I feel the momentum finally collect my weight and drag me into the shallows but I'm too heavy and it soon lets me go. I finish ten yards behind Harrison.

He jumps up in the waist-high water, laughing. 'I win! Come on! Let's do it again!'

I stand up and look towards the flags. James is watching us from the beach, water washing up around his knees. I wave to him and he motions me to join him. He appears uneasy, not distressed but I decide to go and check. I call to Harrison, 'I'll be there in a sec. James wants me'.

Harrison's shoulders drop. He rolls his eyes in exasperation. 'No, Dad! You gotta catch another wave!' The older he gets the less patience he has for anything or anyone, especially me and James.

'You go back out. I'll be there soon.' I lift myself up and stride out of the surf.

James is watching Harrison plunging beneath the crashing wash, swimming out to the smooth water beyond, to the clear rolling humps. 'Dad, if you take me out there you're not allowed to let go of me.'

'No, I won't let go.'

'Promise?'

'Yes, I promise.' I wonder if James has found some courage, or whether his fear of being alone, left behind on the beach, has overcome his fear of being in sea water that is over his head. I decide if one fear makes you overcome another, it is courage.

He holds my wrist with both hands as we walk out into the foaming surf. I lift him up, over the breaking waves, and hold him tight to my body. I carry him through the surf until the water reaches my chest and the waves are slamming into us. Grasping him by the wrist, I drag him over the top of the cresting waves until we're rising up and down on the smooth swell. James has his arms around my neck as we rise and fall, treading water.

Harrison swims over to us. 'Let's all catch a wave together! James! You got to try to beat Dad!'

'No, I just want to stay here for a bit,' and James lets go of my neck with one hand.

I'm treading water with one arm. The other arm is under James, holding him up. 'I'll help put you on a wave if you like.'

'Not a big one'.

'No, not a big one.'

We rise and fall for a while, waiting for the right wave, before Harrison starts pointing out to sea and shouting at us. 'This one! This one!'

The next wave through is short and sharp and raises a clean face before us. 'Okay guys! This one!' I hold James steady as he thrashes his skinny arms and legs. I push him onto the wave. It immediately grabs hold of his small weight and hurls him towards the beach. The wave charges past and I lose sight of him.

I raise my head, pushing myself out of the water, trying to see through the other swimmers. I can't see either boy. Another wave rolls past me. I still can't see them. Then Harrison lifts himself up out of the shallows, shaking his head and looking around for James. He can't see him either.

There! I spot James. My shoulders relax. The wave has taken him all the way to the beach. He pushes himself up out of knee-deep water. He turns to us laughing and yelling, running back out into the foaming wash. I swim in to meet him.

'I win! I beat Harrison! Put me on another one, Dad!'

Harrison says nothing.

I carry James back over the crashing swell and together we swim out through the white water to the clear blue sea beyond. We keep catching waves until we are all tired and trudging across the hot white sand with slumped shoulders. Towels wrapped around our necks, we slowly idle towards the showers of the Greenmount Surf Club.

We return to the beach the next morning. The three of us slowly walking over the squeaking white sand under a glowing sun. Harrison is bare-chested, his t-shirt tucked into the back of his board shorts. James is holding my hand. I drop our large canvas beach bag between the flags and we kick off our thongs.

Harrison tosses his t-shirt to me. He doesn't look back as he runs into the water. 'I'm going for a swim!'

I look down at James. He is watching his older brother swim out into the surf. 'Hey little fella, do you want to dig a tunnel together?'

He keeps his eyes on his older brother. 'I want to go swimming with Harrison.'

I stop. I'm not sure where I am. 'Are you sure? You don't want to build a sandcastle first?'

'I want you to take me swimming with Harrison.' James turns and looks up at me, his large dark eyes uncertain. 'But if you want, I'll build a sandcastle with you.'

'No, that's okay. We can go swimming. I don't need to build a sandcastle,' I say, my parental mask of self-assurance hiding my dismay.

James takes me by the hand and leads me down the beach. He leads me past the toddlers in their sunsuits with their plastic buckets and spades. He leads me past the squealing children splashing in the shallows with their bright plastic kick boards. He leads me past all the sandcastles. Together we swim out past the swirling white water, plunging under the curling foam. We swim to where Harrison is waiting for us, treading water, rising and falling on the smooth glassy humps rolling out of the great blue Pacific Ocean beyond.

Ever since that day, our time at the beach has been about time in the sea. Together we lie on our backs treading water, rising and falling on the soft undulating swell. Staring up at the sky, or looking out to the horizon, waiting for a tall, clear rising wave that will shoot us all back towards the beach.

I stopped asking James if he wanted to build sandcastles. If he wants me to build sandcastles with him he will ask me. But it appears that, for my little men, the hours spent with me as we dribble wet sand through our fingers, building spires and walls, moats and towers, tunnels and mountains, and laughing as we watch the incoming tide wash them away, are behind them.

And for me? My sandcastle days are over.

A HESSIAN DRESS

Wil Roach

The town of Arima is located on the island of Trinidad, nestled in the Caribbean Sea with the Atlantic Ocean to its back. It is known to the local indigenous people, the Arawak, as 'place of water' and sits in the shadow of a mighty mountain range where the Italian explorer, Christopher Columbus, may have imagined that Christ's cross was etched into the landscape. With seemingly little self-doubt, he named the island La Isla de la Trinidad [The Trinity] and it is now simply known as 'Trinidad'. The indigenous people knew the island as 'Lere', meaning 'Land of the Hummingbird'.

Christopher Columbus arrived there in 1498 on his third Spanish exploration funded by King Ferdinand and Queen Isabella to find the fabled lands of India, which they believed held many riches. He landed without hindrance from the Arawak, who had been settled on the island for as long as any could remember. They were unaware (some might say it was a blessing) of how their lives would eventually be devastated by the arrival of this motley crew of sailors, soldiers and bounty hunters, when their land first belonged to a country which they knew nothing about.

Columbus's intention was to achieve three things: to find gold, and water, and something to seal the hulls of his leaking ships. The first condition would satisfy the demands of his royal master and mistress and the second would mean his men could survive. The third would allow his expedition to complete its exploration. But Columbus found no gold on this part of his voyage, though he found water. Alas, he had to make do with the West Indies, rather than far-flung India, never returning to the island after the completion of the voyage.

Some four hundred and fourteen years later, Columbus was the last person on the mind of one of the Arawaks' descendants, Miss Joanie, nor how her people came to be dispossessed of their land.

In 1912, she was living in Arima and she didn't know about the Spanish strangers who'd arrived centuries before. It had not been in the interests of the British who'd seized the island in 1797 to teach the scattered Arawaks about how, as Columbus's colonial successors, they had dispersed the clans.

One thing Miss Joanie had been thinking about recently was how hard her life had been and still was. She knew this February day, just before the annual Carnival Mas, that whatever a woman's beauty – and in her case this was her petite stature, straight dark hair and pretty face, rounded off with light skin and white teeth – she had enough to attract any man; this she knew from experience.

Yet she also knew that this had not been of any help for her or her children in recent years. As her mother, Ma Toots, would say, looking straight at her so that she felt as naked as the day she'd been born, 'No man will ever look after another man's child and that's that.'

Miss Joanie knew that if she got into a mess, she'd have to get herself out of it 'by hook or by crook,' as the old people would say, but she reflected sourly that it was alright for them as they were already dead and gone.

Joanie inhabited the ground floor set of rooms in a very old bar-rack house, one that had formerly held captured slaves long before she was born. In fact, she heard mention from her mother, as far back as the 1830s.

The house, mercifully, had a small verandah, a lime pit toilet in the back and a patch of muddy earth front and back, with very little vegetation. Its metal galvanised roof had aged into a dark muddy colour, and though it provided some protection from the heat of the unforgiving rays of the summer's sun, it was still unbearable to be indoors when the heat struck at midday.

The house had a commodious indoor kitchen and two small bedrooms, though it often felt cramped to Joanie.

'Ah well,' she would sigh as she prepared to hang out the day's washing before the sun made its presence felt.

In order to earn what she called a 'light dusting of money' to meet her basic needs, she would take in clothing to wash from the local wealthy white families. She wasn't proud of herself for having to do this but what else could she do? With a husband dead and his children to be fed. Her man for ten years, Mr Roy, had expired without warning one bright yet sad morning a year before.

After he'd passed, she'd struggled to find enough for all of them to eat, even though she'd taken in washing. This was the only work that was available to a woman in her situation, as she had not completed her formal colonial schooling beyond the age of seven. So her prospects were bleak.

Joanie knew the money from being a washer woman was a poor use of her intelligence, let alone being back-breaking work. As she considered doing without a man and making it on her own she knew she had little choice. No man, no money, and starvation may have seemed inevitable, but placing the children with relatives was in her view the only option.

At approximately 4 pm, before the calm afternoon breeze had subsided, Big Man – short, squat, muscular and 'black as the ace of spades', as the expression went – would appear, to collect that day's washing – dry, clean and fresh for delivery to its white owners before dusk.

When observing Big Man in the past, Joanie had noticed that she had a less than healthy interest in him, his bull neck of thick flesh like a protective carapace and a hard as nails attitude to match. She knew he did piece work on one of the surviving plantations but although she needed a new man, this one was not to her taste, and she had cast her eye elsewhere.

It was plain that the money from washing wasn't enough for her to live on. So she decided that a man with whom she was recently acquainted, Mr John John, would do. A tall serious-looking man, he had a market garden not far from her barracks house where he grew all manner of vegetables. One afternoon, some time after Mr Roy died, he asked Miss Joanie, while they were liming in the town square, if she was interested in him. Her heartbeat quickened. 'Yes,' she replied, still a little circumspect. She was cautious, knowing she had to tread delicately due to her undisclosed pregnancy. His face was a mixture of puzzlement and strength. She liked what his face told her about his strength and he seemed to be a man of few words. This would be okay if he was also a man of few questions but, if not, she was in trouble. Despite what her mother had said, she decided to take the plunge.

When Ma Toots, a woman who the whole town knew had 'a mouth that had no cover' (that is, showed no respect for the living or dead) queried yet again why Joanie needed a man around her, in fact any man, Joanie replied with fury, 'You know! Without a man we'd starve.'

Her mother's silence left Joanie bitter. She knew her mother was condemning her, but what right did she have to say this to her own daughter? Joanie knew what state she'd found herself in when Mr Roy, the father of her three children – Joan, John and Jess – had died without warning. Penniless.

When her mother went for her with her viciousness, Joanie wanted to scream in her mother's unmoved face about how she hadn't even had time to grieve.

Yet she thought better of it when she remembered that her eldest daughter, Joan, had been placed with her sister, Mildred, and her boy John had gone with his grandmother. Her youngest, Jess, aged six, had been placed in the Home for Wayward Boys and Girls, located just outside Arima.

Of her three children, Jess was the most troublesome. She was apt to defy Joanie without reason and to behave as if she were three times her age. Joanie used to sigh that if only Mr Roy had survived, surely none of the worries that befell her after his death would have come to pass.

She had grown fearful when, not long after he died, she realised she was pregnant with his baby. *Well*, she thought, *salvation is at hand.* But the price, it seemed to her, was sometimes too heavy. To end the turmoil in her mind, she hung her head down, wanting to cry, and whispered to herself, 'What to do?'

It pained Joanie to admit that, 'The apple hadn't fallen far from the tree,' when it came to her having children, just as her mother had had several unplanned pregnancies.

One afternoon, preoccupied with these thoughts, suddenly, with urgency, she grabbed the white sheets, folding and re-folding them as she'd realised the time and knew that they needed to be dry and ready for collection when the white owners' servant, Big Man, arrived, or she wouldn't be paid.

Then, as if some fright to the core of her being had taken place, she whispered to herself, 'Get a hold of yourself! Leave the sheets to dry and pray this quiet man will do the trick, because something has to change – and fast.'

Once the sheets were dry, basically from the heat of the day, Joanie finished folding them. She took armsful and briefly smelt them for her handiwork, telling herself that whatever anyone thought of her, at least her sheets would always be the whitest and cleanest in the town.

With that she hurried indoors to await the arrival of Big Man.

Not long after, there was a bass voice richly lubricated with dark rum. It was Big Man, who called out, 'Joanie, Joanie, you there?' Without replying, she collected the sheets and thrust them at him. He smiled without saying another word to her. So she stuck out a slightly discoloured hand, silently demanding her monetary reward for her toil. In a silent reply, he fished out of his pocket a fistful of dollars and pushed them into her palm, without flesh touching flesh, and departed as fast as he could. *As if he's leaving a disciple of the devil*, she thought.

At last Joanie felt she could relax, and with that idea she dropped into her favourite verandah chair with an audible *Bam*! She didn't care. Her legs felt like the rough ground she'd tramped over to hang and retrieve the linen from the line. She wondered if her tiredness might be due to the baby but pushed that thought away. She folded her arms, her eyes scanning the road as if expecting someone. Joanie began to grow uneasy. She did not invite suspense nor bid it to stay long if it should happen to turn up unannounced. The absence of any animal or discernible human presence around her humble abode unsettled her.

A feeling of an unannounced visitor due any moment led her to wonder whether it was her oldest daughter Joan, living with Mildred, who might be on her way. Yet she knew that wasn't how it should be done. Normally, Joanie would get a message by word of mouth giving her a warning of her daughter's impending arrival.

While scanning the verandah she looked down and saw in a large basket, something she was ashamed to admit she'd created with her own hands.

It was a dress, cut and made from a rough heavy material used to pack refined sugar for export to Britain, which former slaves had found a use for as a protection from the blistering heat of the sun when outdoors, cutting cane on the plantation. It was known as hessian and it signified to Joanie how poor she had become, because if worn in public it would be a sign of her shame. She realised, on reflection, that in a moment of panic after Mr Roy had died, she'd made it for Jess. She'd been too ashamed to admit out loud to anyone that she didn't want Mr John John to think that she'd lavish his money on the child of another man. Maybe she left it out to prove that if by chance Jess should return from the Home then not a penny would be spent on her. At least John John would understand that. Wouldn't he?

As Joanie sat weighing these painful thoughts, the familiar figure of Miss Goat, one of Joanie's most visible neighbours, appeared as if out of the unforgiving ground. She'd come by that name, being the keeper of a small herd of black goats, a woman of dark hue and sparse words yet observant.

Today her head was wrapped in an old towel, reminding Joanie of the slave women her mother used to describe to her, those who had lived on the former plantation where Mr Roy had worked. It seemed to Joanie that slavery was now performed by another name without the inconvenience of Man's conscience.

'Oh, God, Miss Joanie, how can you stand to be out in this heat?' Miss Goat shouted out to the reclining Joanie, who didn't reply but regarded the other woman as a nuisance, yet a useful distraction from her uncomfortable thoughts.

She didn't want to say anything that would create an unfavourable impression that would be sure to reach her mother's ears, so she coolly answered, 'Yes, Miss Goat, it sure is hot like the devil stretching himself but I am alright!'

Then, as if Miss Goat sensed Joanie's underlying unease, she announced, 'I see some little girl in town this morning.'

At these words Jeanie jumped up as if propelled by the forceful push of an unseen hand. She went to speak but nothing left her now parched, dry mouth.

'Yes,' Miss Goat continued, answering a question that had not been asked, 'it was Jess I saw this morning, but didn't have a chance to ask her why she was in Arima.'

Joanie wanted to hear no more and rushed inside her house, slamming the door.

Not long after, as Joanie lay on her bed counting her fears out one by one as to what this disastrous development might portend, she realised that Miss Goat had seen Jess that morning and it was now 2 pm. Joanie calculated that Jess might by now be in mortal danger. Where was Jess?

She was about to prepare herself to try and head off a calamity before Mr John John returned home, when she heard a knock at the door. Her heart hadn't stopped but it felt like it had, and she couldn't move from the spot. Then again, *knock, knock*. The softness of the knock confirmed Joanie's worst fears. The knocks were those of a child.

Joanie slowly moved towards the door, and stood waiting. Then another *knock, knock*. She rushed to open the door, pulling it with a vigour that almost saw it leave its hinges.

There stood her daughter. Joanie gasped, her hand covering her mouth but no tears, as she absorbed her daughter's features as if they were being acquainted for the first time. Jess's small round face, dark hair pulled back, and clothes filthy from the walk, spoke to Joanie of the fact that she must have walked all the way home in the blazing sun.

Dear God!' Joanie exclaimed, before pushing past the little bundle of innocence to the basket containing the dress, grabbing it and thrusting it at Jess, as she shouted, 'Put this on now and then we will walk all the way back to the Children's Home. I have no money. I told you not to do this!' She was screaming, barely able to contain her fury and fear. 'Hurry, hurry. We need to leave now! Girl, what have you done?'

Jess did not reply because she was afraid and exhausted, as she changed out of her dirty clothes and donned the hessian dress, which fitted her well. Her mother had hoped she'd never have to use it.

She told Jess, in a tone that could shatter a fragile object let alone the spirit of a six year old, to sit still on a chair, while she hurriedly prepared herself with a change of clothing, a bottle of water and some fruit hastily stuffed into a straw bag.

Joanie calculated that it would take a couple of hours for them to get to the Home before dark. She left a scribbled note for John John, knowingly lying as she wrote, 'I received word that Jess is unwell and will visit her now and return tomorrow. I will stay with Mildred. Please don't worry.' She folded the letter neatly and placed it under the clock.

Joanie found an old coat and dusted it off, coughing. She ensured it wasn't too tight, then put it on. She and Jess strode out of the house into the cooling sunshine as if they didn't have a care in the world.

She held the little girl's hand with a cruelty that belied her own fear. The fear of being found out by John John. The fear of being unable to cope, of collapsing and not being able to get up. Jess tried to escape her mother's suffocating grip but it was to no avail.

After what seemed like hours, the lights of the Home came into view. By then the mother and daughter were both clearly exhausted, having walked for miles, refusing all offers of lifts from friendly donkey cart owners.

Joanie's fury knew no bounds. As they approached the Home's arched metal gate, with its title 'Wayward Boys and Girls' etched into the ageing metal, an undeclared war had opened up between them.

Joanie at first pushed Jess towards the wooden entrance of the Home but stopped at the steps, as if wondering who was really the wayward party in this unfolding and unequal war. Yet she knew there was no turning back. It was either Jess or her, and she sure as hell was going to make sure it wasn't her!

With no motherly love to offer, she shouted at the quivering girl, 'Don't you ever do that again. Never leave this place. Do you hear? Do you hear me?'

Jess shook, as she had no words to explain her grief.

The end for both of them was in sight.

Joanie pushed the little girl again, up the steps towards the dark entrance of the Home. Jess did not turn to look at her mother as she slipped in through the large wooden doors that now sealed her fate.

With those last harsh words from Joanie, neither knew it then, but in that moment both mother and daughter were lost to each other forever.

AUTHORS

DAVID BENN

David was born in Gatton, Queensland in 1967 and attended St Joseph's College Nudgee before completing a Bachelor of Business at the Queensland University of Technology.

Graduating in the midst of a declining economic environment, he moved to Sydney looking for work and briefly followed a career in banking and finance. A redundancy gave him the opportunity to buy a house or travel. David chose to travel.

Returning to Sydney, David pursued a career in jewellery, buying the old family company Arthur C Easy & Son in 2001. David has two sons and claims a string of old girlfriends.

GABRIELA DIMITROVA

Gabriela is interested in reading and writing in the poetry and short story genres, particularly historical fiction and fantasy.

A professionally trained nurse, Gabriela is completing a Postgraduate Diploma in Creative Writing and Literature at Deakin University, and working on a collection of short stories which explores a range of historical times, people and places.

KAY DUNNE

As a child, Kay imagined being a writer, living in a cosy cottage in the bushland of the Blue Mountains. Although this hasn't quite eventuated, Kay considers her first career as an actor tuned her perception to the rhythm and nuances of words and story-telling.

She has had several stories published in the mainstream press, and holds a degree in English literature and drama, as well as a Master of Fine Arts in Creative Writing.

LAWRENCE GOODSTONE

Lawrence is a retired public servant who spent his professional life writing for others. With a background in teaching, adult corrections, immigrant services and assisting in the delivery of the 2000 Olympic Games in Sydney, he is now in a position to write for himself and create stories from a life well lived.

RICHARD HAMBLETON

Richard has published a number of short stories, and won both first prize and third prize in Victoria's The Age Readings Short Story Competition 2013.
He was hired as an advertising writer at the age of 20 and later built and eventually sold an advertising agency. Richard now lives with wife Margie in Hepburn Springs, Victoria.

JODY HARPER

A keen reader and lover of words, Jody is currently in the process of writing a memoir. She's had work published previously in local newspapers and most recently was shortlisted in a 'Better Read Than Dead' writing competition. Her style has been described as raw and real, penetrating people's emotions.
Jody hopes to raise people's awareness and claims her greatest joy is when she is 'self-expressed' via writing.

SAM HERZOG

Sam is a psychology graduate from the University of Sydney.
Since completing his studies, he has opted to pursue a career in creative writing. Due to this, he has had no real employment, so if you know of something please get in touch, he suggests.

CAROLE INGRAM

Carole's imagination took wings as a child when she discovered magical fairy stories. At school, when a love of reading and writing was born in her mind, she enjoyed writing compositions with exciting characters.
She has published a personal account of Alzheimer's disease and the heartache caused within a family unit. Carole's love of philosophical writing and poetry also led her to self-publish 'Visions', which was written in a similar style to the famous 'Desiderata'.

MATT JACKSON

Growing up in Newcastle, north of Sydney, Matt was described as a boy with an imagination bigger than that allowed by the space of his head. As an adult he splits his time between a professional services career and various creative pursuits.

He says he writes to explore the raw human experience, and seeks to 'challenge the nature of the bond formed between character and reader'.

JENNIFER NEIL

Jennifer was born in Edinburgh, Scotland and, along with her identical twin sister, was adopted as a baby and taken to South Africa. She became politically active against the apartheid regime there and left in 1960 for England.

She has lived in Australia since 1963 and describes herself as a feminist, lesbian, environmentalist and a loving Nana.

THEO PERRY

Born in Singapore, Theo was raised in Australia and has spent the last thirty years travelling throughout the United States. His primary career focus has been in the beauty industry.

Theo looks to writing as a vehicle of expression that allows for flexibility and creative freedom. He says one of his aims is to create characters as a vehicle to explore human behaviour, for example, the many ways a character may overcome negative internal messaging in facing obstacles in life.

JIM PIOTROWSKI

Jim lives in Erskineville, where he is writing a book about a paranoid detective, who's not really a detective and probably not even properly paranoid.

He won this year's 'Better Read Than Dead' winter writing competition.

MICHELLE PORTER

Michelle has loved books since she was a child, reading whenever it was possible to find stories with 'that inexplicable magic'. She majored in Writing for an Arts Degree at Southern Cross University. In Sydney working in a book store, she began to write arts reviews and features.

Currently, she works as a librarian and yoga teacher.

WIL ROACH

Wil had a culturally diverse start in life, born in Trinidad before his parents migrated to London in the early '60s. He grew up within a rich Trinidadian and English immigrant experience of interdependent identities spanning culture, race and sexuality.

Wil says his primary London experiences provided him with a deep well to draw on for his first book in a trilogy of memoir, Black, Gay & Underage, published by Sydney School of Arts & Humanities in early 2019. He has also had poems published in a collection by the group, 'Poetry at the Sydney Mechanics School of Arts', and a story included in 'Living and Loving in Diversity'.

PATRICIA RUELL

Patricia worked in a science research laboratory for many years and contributed to several scientific publications in peer reviewed journals.

She lives near the Georges River with her family, including her cat named Juno. Among several short stories she has published is The Rose-print *Dress*, which won first prize in a 'Discovery Writers' memoir competition.

Patricia is inspired by places she has visited on her travels.

FAISAL SAYANI

Faisal is currently studying towards a Master of Arts in Creative Writing & Literary Studies at UWS, with a project to research the life of a Pakistani political activist. This involves a questioning of the

revisionist history of Pakistan to 'set the record straight'.
Previously, as executive producer and head of programming at the Pakistani television news networks (DawnNews and Express News) he established and managed a number of documentary, current affairs, news, entertainment and special events transmissions.

GRAHAM WILSON

Graham has self-published twelve books, including a memoir and two nov*el series, the Old Balmain House Series and a psychological thriller set in the Australian outback, the Crocodile Dreaming Series.*
Graham is now a resident of Sydney but lived and worked in the Northern Territory for the first half of his life. His books reflect this experience, including growing up in an Aboriginal community and surviving attack by a large crocodile.
Graham writes for creative pleasure and says he is particularly gratified when any unknown person enjoys one of his stories and lets him know.